# P.C. HAWKE
## mysteries

DISCARDED # THE
# SCREAM
# MUSEUM

- - - - - - - -

## PAUL ZINDEL

## VOLO

Hyperion
New York

To Donna and Shannon—
the cunning and judicious Watsons
of my murderous ink.
—P.Z.

Copyright © 2001 by Paul Zindel

Volo and the Volo colophon are trademarks of Disney Enterprises, Inc.
All rights reserved. No part of this book may be reproduced or transmitted in
any form or by any means, electronic or mechanical, including photocopying,
recording, or by any information storage and retrieval system, without written
permission from the publisher. For information address Volo Books,
114 Fifth Avenue, New York, New York 10011-5690.

First Edition
1 3 5 7 9 10 8 6 4 2

The text for this book is set in Janson Text 11.5/15.
Photo of thunderstorm: Don Farrall

Library of Congress Catalog Card Number on file.
ISBN 0-7868-1572-8
Visit www.volobooks.com

## Acknowledgments

To David and Lizabeth, my favorite sleuths, for the flesh and fearlessness of my heroes P.C. Hawke and Mackenzie Riggs

To P.C. McPhee, the namesake and young champion from my novel *Reef of Death* (HarperCollins, Hyperion) To Mike Mencotti for cunningly bestowing a last name on P.C. Hawke.

To the many educators, librarians, and media specialists, their schools, and their fab and brill students who inspired me and helped me sleuth this book into being: Teri Lesesne; Jami Hradecky, Anne Hage, Wanda Clement, Jackie Snowden, Lisa Churchill, Mary Marks, Randy LaLonde, Marjorie Lohr, Cheryl Sigmon, Debbie Cooke, Sue Malaska, Donna Moody, Cheri Estes, and to Arleen Perkins and her *Sixth-grade sweetie pies* (Egads, this is a partial list!)

# Contents

| | | |
|---|---|---|
| 1 | Reading, Writing, and Code 1 | 3 |
| 2 | Corpse Time | 9 |
| 3 | Freak of Nature | 17 |
| 4 | Tombs and Duck Sauce | 26 |
| 5 | Life at the Morgue | 33 |
| 6 | Megabyting a Murderer | 43 |
| 7 | Exploring | 49 |
| 8 | Mummy Dearest | 55 |
| 9 | Hexes, Lies, and Videotape | 63 |
| 10 | Greed | 76 |
| 11 | A Stalk in the Park | 86 |
| 12 | Attack | 96 |
| 13 | Sticks and Stones | 103 |
| 14 | A Worm Is the Only Animal That Can't Fall Down | 110 |
| 15 | Evil Eye | 120 |
| 16 | Making a Killing | 136 |
| 17 | Death Is Nature's Way of Saying "Howdy" | 144 |

# THE
# SCREAM
# MUSEUM

# THE SCREAM MUSEUM • Case #1

## Case #1 began something like this:

1) On Friday, September 23, at exactly 2:43 in the afternoon, an earsplitting scream rose from a laboratory on the lower level of New York City's Museum of Natural History.

2) A monsignor and seven nuns from Our Lady Star of the Sea convent were checking out the sixty-three-foot-long canoe in the Northwest Indian exhibit and heard the scream.

3) A tourist couple from Tokyo said they were examining the Giant Mosquito Model in the Hall of Biology and thought the shriek had come from the animated T. Rex exhibit on the fourth floor.

4) A weird eighth-grade class from the Bronx High School of Science was sketching the Visible Woman Hologram and thought somebody had gotten hit by a car on Central Park West.

Soon, however, all would discover that the scream they'd heard was the last breath of Dr. Conchetta Farr, the museum's head of research. What's more to the point is that I (Peter Christopher Hawke, whose notebook this is) and my pal, Mackenzie Riggs, would quickly find ourselves smack in the middle of a puzzling and vicious murder case.

Recording the truth and nothing but the truth,

I am

*P. C. Hawke*

(a.k.a. Peter Christopher Hawke)

## Reading, Writing, and Code 1

**An hour after the grisly death of Dr. Farr**, Mackenzie and I heard about it. We were five blocks south, sitting in our junior English class at Westside School, a private academy for kids who are sort of privileged, gifted, or freaky. The most privileged one's father owns half of the Chrysler Building and all of the Rockettes; the most gifted kid is in the Rand Corporation think tank for space travel; and the freakiest is a sophomore who plays electric guitar and has been nursing her pet ferret that's been in a coma for three years. There are a lot of off-the-wall, strange, and way-out characters at Westside, too—and that's just the faculty.

Anyway, the bell had rung for everyone to meander from their seventh- to their eighth-period class. I leaped to my feet, threw my loose-leaf binder into my orange backpack, and grunted my way out of Miss Conlan's class. Yes, I am a grunter. When I don't like things, I make sounds like *egads, jeez, ummh, holy kamozes,* and *gar-ruuunt*.

What I was ticked off about at the moment was that

Spalding Kazinski had weaseled his way into teaming up with me and my buddy Mackenzie on our English class folklore project. And I knew exactly why he wanted the three of us chosen to research the Indian god Ganesh.

"Egads," I said, running my fingers through the spikes of my gelled hair. "Even as a freshman Kazinski was a calculating goofus."

Mackenzie picked up her pace to keep close to me as I zigzagged my way from Miss Conlan's classroom and through the mob of kids in the hallway. "Well, Miss Conlan set the teams, so we'll have to make the best of it. He just told her he admires us and that he's always been fascinated by Indian religion and folklore."

"Well, I think he's a big phony. All he did was read in the papers that my dad's museum's just received the Ganesh necklace from India, so he thinks hanging out with us is going to have a lot of perks." My dad is Dr. Stephen Hawke, one of the top archaeologists in the country and head of archaeology at the Museum of Natural History.

Mackenzie checked to make certain her cat's-eye sunglasses were still wedged onto the top of her head, trapping her long blond hair. "I think the tackiest thing Kazinski ever did was wear black vinyl pants and a T-shirt that said 'No, I didn't escape—I'm on a day pass' to the Student Council meeting."

I jumped when I felt something twitching in my back pocket. I remembered I'd left my cell phone on vibrate.

I took the phone out, flicked down its mouthpiece, and hit the answer key. From the ID screen I knew the call was from my best guy friend, Jesus.

"What's up?"

Jesus Lopez's high-pitched voice crackled with static. "Where's your father?"

I stopped at a bank of windows on one side of the hall-way near a display case that housed a collection of weird student-made puppet heads and clay vases imbedded with chunks of gaudy costume jewelry. "Why?"

"Just tell me."

"He left yesterday to help carbon-date bones in Sumatra."

"Good," Jesus said. "Then it's not him."

"What are you talking about?"

"A Code-One for the museum just came over the police radio band. Squad cars are heading there now."

Even though my dad had been gone for a week, I was worried anyway. Code-One was police shorthand for homicide. "Thanks, Jesus. We'll check into it."

I closed my phone, shoved it back into the pocket of my chinos, and spun on my heels. "Bad news at the museum."

"What's up?" Mackenzie asked.

"Someone's just been murdered. What do you say we duck out early and head uptown?"

"Let's do it," Mackenzie said. She put her assignment pad away into the fake-leopard shoulder bag that she'd recently bought for three dollars in a SoHo thrift shop, and followed me to the main office. I used my irresistible smile and soothing voice on Miss Xanthe, the bleached-blond secretary, to snag two early-dismissal passes. I was truthful, saying that there was an emergency at my father's workplace. I just left out the part about Dad being away on the other side of the planet.

Spalding Kazinski came running up to us as we were heading for the exit. He had one of his "oh, let me suck up to you some more" expressions on his face. "I wanted to warn you guys that Wendy Fillerman's been gossiping about the two of you again," Spalding said.

"What's she saying this time?" Mackenzie pretended she was interested.

"She came up to me during family living class," Spalding said, "and warned me, 'Oh, don't invite P.C. Hawke or Mackenzie Riggs to any party of yours or you're going to end up having Cokes, egg rolls, and a big, fresh corpse.' Isn't that mean?"

"Thanks, Spalding," Mackenzie said, in her special way that means get lost.

"I'm really looking forward to working with you both on Ganesh!" he called after us as we practically ran away from him.

We left Westside School and cut across the street and past the Texas Barbecue and Oliver Cromwell Hotel. The Dakota apartment house on the corner of 72nd and Central Park West loomed like a boxy, Gothic castle.

Neither I nor Mackenzie could ever walk past the Dakota without remembering the horror movie filmed there, in which Mia Farrow gives birth to a demonic baby, and that John Lennon had been shot dead on the walkway in front. I know some people who think ghouls haunt the Dakota. Every building in New York held some dark, freak-of-nature history, it seemed. Now we were on our way to find out about another horror.

"Lucky your father's off on a travel gig," Mackenzie said. I knew this was Mackenzie's way of letting me know she understood what I was feeling. I'd already lost one parent and was often worried about losing the only other one I had left. My mom had died of cancer just after Christmas the year before while my dad was away on a dig in China. Sometimes the feeling of being alone is terrifying.

I think what my mother's dying taught me was how precious a human life is. Ever since, whenever I hear of anyone being cheated out of their life by someone else I want the guilty one to be punished—and who the guilty one is often a mystery. I like solving crimes as much as my dad has always loved solving the mysteries of the world that lie in fossils and ancient temples and distant planets. You might say we're just different *kinds* of detectives.

"You're 'ummh'-ing again," Mackenzie said.

"I guess I am," I said. I often 'ummh' when I'm deep in thought. Mackenzie and I picked up our pace past the

Art Sanctuary and flapping banners that announced its latest photography exhibit, LYNCHINGS IN AMERICA.

At 77th Street, the Museum of Natural History rose before us like an otherworldly stone fortress. It is surrounded on its two-block tract by long stretches of iron fences and gates. The walls of its main buildings are thick granite blocks that rise five stories into the air. It is a massive complex of roomy turrets, flying buttresses, and really vicious-looking gargoyles.

Police cars and emergency vehicles with flashing red lights were parked helter-skelter on the vast cobblestone driveway that swept down to the stone staircases that framed the side entrance to the museum. Both Mackenzie and I recognized the unmarked dark coroner's van with its black windows.

"Somebody's really dead, all right," Mackenzie said.

"Yes," I agreed. "Let's find out *who*. I hope your mother's the coroner on this one."

"I hope not," Mackenzie said. "Thank God, she said she had to do autopsies all day. If she found out I ducked out of school early she'd slice *me* up."

## 2

### Corpse Time

**I led the way** toward the museum's main entrance just across from Central Park. There was the usual ebb and flow of tourists and school groups on the sweep of the front steps. No one seemed aware of the blazing gaggle of police cars at the side entrance, nor that somewhere inside the labyrinthine clutch of buildings there was a crime scene.

We went in through the revolving doors. A red-faced and exhausted-looking Max Durning was standing near the security office, keeping an eye on the crowd.

"Max," I said, "what happened?"

Max let out a groan that rose from the depths of his stocky, short-legged body. "You don't want to know."

"We heard there was a murder," I said. "Who?"

Max hesitated, looking around to make certain no one else was listening. "That little tough woman. You know, the head of research—the Bug Lady."

"Dr. Farr?" I said, amazed.

"Yeah. She was strangled smack in her office," Max mumbled. "But you didn't hear it from me."

"Don't worry, Max. Anyway, it'll be all over the news soon enough," I said. I felt a deep anguish turning inside of me. Mackenzie and I always feel awful when we hear of the death of a human being.

Max's walkie-talkie squawked. He spun away from Mackenzie and me and mumbled some response into it, then called over his shoulder, "Stay out of it, P.C." I guess I've already earned a reputation for being a buttinski.

As Max took off down the hall, he looked like some sort of a pygmy rhino, with his big head and thick neck thrust forward, his nose veins broken from high blood pressure or too much beer. Mackenzie and I zipped after him, giving a nod to Mrs. Ebb who was taking tickets and checking annual passes. The dizzying Theodore Roosevelt rotunda hovered over a central marble fountain and fern garden. A moment later we were scooting after Max through the Hall of North American Mammals.

"Who'd want to kill Dr. Farr?" Mackenzie asked me.

"Probably half of the two hundred people who work at the museum," I said. "Dad talked about her a lot at dinner. He said she had the power to control everyone's research grants, and if you didn't suck up to her big-time, she'd nail you to the floor like a French duck. She could make or break a career around here—arrange it so you could publish *and* perish. How weird that she's the one who has perished."

"Max, who do you think killed her?" Mackenzie asked as we caught up to him.

"We already caught the killer—got him red-handed with his fingers around Conchetta's throat." Another jumble blared from the walkie-talkie. Max mumbled into the mouthpiece again as he charged onward with his tiny frantic steps.

"Who?" I asked.

"Boggs," Max said.

"Boggs?" Mackenzie and I blurted together, shocked and disturbed. "*Tom* Boggs?"

"Yeah. The assistant custodian."

"That's absurd," Mackenzie said. "We know Tom Boggs. He's a nice guy! He wouldn't hurt a mosquito."

"That's what I thought," Max said. "Then today, just before three, I heard this horrible scream. Two tourists from Cleveland and I ran down Hallway C and saw Tommy Boy strangling the Bug Lady. There were a couple of other witnesses, too." Max hurried around a corner past a stuffed walrus and the Mollusks of Our World exhibit, and rushed down into a stairwell. Mackenzie and I followed.

The lower level had the museum food court, loads of big storerooms, a passage to the parking garage, and the main lobby for the planetarium. Shooting off the planetarium lobby were a half dozen wide hallways leading to the south wing research labs and offices.

Dr. Grant Gardner, the museum's director, was standing

at a police barricade blocking the entrance to Hallway C. He was dressed impeccably, as usual, in a dark suit and tie, and was explaining the situation to several members of the staff who wanted to get back to their offices. "Not right now," Gardner was telling everyone. "We have a problem. . . ."

Gardner took Max aside, whispered instructions into his ear, and sent him scurrying off toward the group of police and detectives milling in and out of Farr's lab. The police photographer's flash-spots were firing every few seconds.

Mackenzie flipped her sunglasses down over her eyes and took out her pad and pencil. "I'll note anything weird or freaky around here."

"Good," I told her. "I'll talk to Gardner."

I walked up to Gardner and got right to the point. "Excuse me, Dr. Gardner, you don't really think Tom Boggs killed Dr. Farr, do you?"

Gardner looked at me. "Peter, I know your dad sponsored Tom for his job here, and that you and Mackenzie were friends with him." Gardner was one of the few of my father's colleagues who still called me Peter.

"We're sort of friends," I said.

The moment the words were out I felt guilty. Everyone knew that Tom was a few pickles short of a barrel. He had an IQ in the nineties, and any of Mackenzie's and my friends from Westside would make fun of him if they heard him talk. But Mackenzie and I believe in the truth of a human face. Just because Tom didn't say much didn't mean he had nothing to say. And it was easy to see in his eyes that he had a good heart. With some people words get in the way. That's how it was with Tom. His every movement said *please like me*.

"I've heard several of the eyewitness accounts myself," Gardner said gently. "I'm afraid Tom did it, all right."

"But why? He had no motive. We've gone with him to the movies. To Serendipity's for frozen hot chocolate. We know him. He had no reason to kill Conchetta Farr or anyone else for that matter."

"I'm very puzzled about this, too," Dr. Gardner said. "Tom must have snapped, like one of those post office employees. One day they're eating their lunches, chatting to everyone, the next they're bringing in a sawed-off shotgun and shooting a half dozen of their coworkers."

"Tom always liked Dr. Farr," I said. I still couldn't believe Tom was the murderer. "She let him feed snacks to her tarantulas and centipedes. Her famous African roaches! She was like a hero to him. He used to cut out articles about her like 'THE BUG LADY GIVES PRAYING MANTIS LECTURE' or 'BUG LADY SPEAKER AT YONKERS KIWANIS.'"

"I didn't know that."

"Tom's favorite spider of hers was Aristotle, the albino tarantula. Dr. Farr would take Aristotle out of her terrarium and let him sit on Tom's hand while he fed it larvae. He loved Conchetta's whole living creepy collection. He wouldn't *strangle* her," I said.

Renée Dell, the assistant museum director, came down the hallway and took over Gardner's job of appeasing the gathering crowd at the barricade. I signaled Mackenzie that I was leaving with Gardner and followed him across the planetarium lobby toward the elevators.

"I understand Farr recently told Tom her lab was off-limits to him," Dr. Gardner said.

"She was trying to breed a pair of Madagascar scorpions and she didn't want them disturbed," I said. "Tom understood. His nose wasn't out of joint. He didn't have a vengeful bone in his body. Besides, nobody knocks off anyone for taking away bug-visiting privileges."

"I'm sorry, Peter," Gardner said, "but I'm afraid that there may be more to this than you know."

The elevator door opened. I got in, but Gardner was stopped outside by Jeffrey Mirsky, the head of the paleontology department. I don't think Mirsky saw me, as he began shooting off his mouth.

"I just want you to understand, Gardner, that I don't expect you to pass me over this time. Farr's position should have been mine the last time around, and I'm not going to let you cheat me out of it again."

"Now wait a minute, Jeff," Dr. Gardner told Mirsky in his calm, smooth voice. "Dr. Farr was awarded her position because she was the most qualified and . . ."

"Baloney!" Mirsky stopped Gardner in midsentence. I had seen Jeffrey Mirsky dominate conversations in the past, even with my father. Mirsky was in his early fifties, and prided himself on being a powerful socialite. As a paleontologist, he was known for identifying prehistoric bones with flair and speed, often at the expense of accuracy.

I saw Beverly Congers, one of the museum's anthropologists, close in on Mirsky and Gardner. I half-hid against the side of the elevator and kept my finger on the "door open" button. Congers was ten years younger than Mirsky, with red hair cut into a shingle.

"Grant," Congers said, completely ignoring Mirsky. "I have the seniority for Conchetta's job. Consider this conversation my application for it."

"You're joking," Mirsky said, turning to face Congers.

"I'm afraid I'm not," Congers said. "I knew you wouldn't let Farr's body get stiff before you'd be making your move."

"Beverly," Mirsky said with a smile, "you're completely underqualified to be head of research. You're absurd."

"You know, Jeffrey," Dr. Congers said, "if you ever changed your faith it'd be because you no longer think you're God."

"You see how she is." Mirsky talked to Gardner as though Congers wasn't even there. "You couldn't have anyone like her in any position that affects the image of the museum. Assigning grants requires tact and diplomacy. She'd walk into a cremation and ask, 'What's cooking?'"

Congers moved so she was right in Mirsky's face. "You're just jealous, Jeffrey, because I'm in *Who's Who* and you're in *Who's Through*!" She turned and took off, her high heels clicking on the marble floor with the insistence of a metronome.

"You know Hawke's boy?" Dr. Gardner asked Mirsky, trying to break the tension. I stepped out of the elevator. Mirsky looked uncomfortably surprised to see me.

"Oh, yes," Mirsky said. He peered over his glasses at me. "You're the one who spotted that dead body in some department store window. That was very observant of you."

"I guess I'm just lucky," I said.

Mirsky turned back to Gardner. "You remember what I told you, Grant."

"Good day, Dr. Mirsky," Gardner said as he stepped into the elevator. I pretended I had heard nothing, and Gardner seemed to prefer it that way.

## 3

## Freak of Nature

**"What should I know about Tom that I don't?"** I asked, trying to get my mind off Mirsky and Congers and back on track.

"I think you need to understand *exactly* what happened today, and then what I have to tell you about Tom will make more sense," Gardner said.

We got off the elevator on the fifth floor and went directly into Dr. Gardner's office. He sat in a space-age swivel chair behind a massive chrome-and-glass desk. The wall directly behind the desk was a sweep of dark mahogany bookshelves crammed with art and history books, many of them leather-bound with gold lettering. The east exposure was a floor-to-ceiling brown-tinted window overlooking Central Park.

I took a seat on a black leather sofa and checked out everything in the room. There was a cluster of framed university degrees and international honors awarded the museum; several family photos including one of Gardner and his wife and children wearing cowpoke gear; a mounted bull's head with horns; and a glass paperweight with a real rabbit's foot frozen in it.

"The thing we're certain of from Max is that Tom was sweeping the lower lobby of the planetarium," Gardner said. "The first 'Death of the Universe' show was ending, you know, with its supernova explosions and music spilling out into the lobby. Max's assistant, Patience, saw that Tom simply laid his broom down and walked calmly toward Hallway C like he was going to get a drink or take a coffee break. Moments later, Max and the other witnesses heard Dr. Farr's scream and ran down Hallway C. It wasn't long—maybe a couple of minutes—before they saw Tom in the doorway of Conchetta's lab. Conchetta was in her desk chair, and he had his hands around her throat and, Max said, a very crazy look in his eyes."

I tried to picture that. "If Tom was a closet psycho, Mackenzie's dad would have picked up on it," I insisted. "Dr. Riggs only treated Tom for mild depression and suggested he eat more blueberries to help punch his IQ up a couple of points. Dr. Riggs was worried about his diet and felt he'd have more focus if he ate the right foods. That's all. There's something wrong with the scenario you described, Dr. Gardner. I know my dad's going to be shocked when he hears about it."

"I don't think so."

I sat forward. "There's more?"

Dr. Gardner looked pained. "Peter, your father and I have discussed Tom. Haven't you or Mackenzie noticed the kind of friends he's been hanging around with lately? From what I've been able to see, Tom's gotten involved with a very bad element."

I thought I knew what Gardner might be getting at. "You think he's doing drugs?"

"It's more complicated than that."

"What?"

"Things have been *missing* from the museum. None of the antiquities. I'm talking about office equipment like a laptop. A radio. A paper shredder! It's the kind of stuff kids steal and can sell or trade easily for drugs." He stood up suddenly and pointed out the window. "That's one of Tom's pals down there now near the wisteria arbor."

At the edge of the park I could see a kid with hair like a greasy chrysanthemum, gray-and-blue camouflage pants pulled down low on his waist, and a torn black T-shirt. His body language reminded me of a nervous, guilty dog. He was looking over everybody who passed down the steps of the arbor in the direction of the 79th Street transverse like he wanted to do a buy or lock in on a mark.

I had seen and heard enough from Gardner to know what Mackenzie and I would have to do next, not the least of which would be to add Mirsky and Congers to the top of our Boy-Do-I-Hate-Conchetta list. "Well, thanks for letting me know about Tom and what's been going on. There are a few of these things I'd like to check out," I said standing up. "I'm very sorry about Dr. Farr, but there's something very wrong with what I'm hearing. The way you described it, Tom was calm. I don't think anyone who's going to strangle someone is *calm*. And what strikes me most strange is the eyewitness reports that he strangled Dr. Farr in the doorway of her lab."

"What do you mean?"

"Strangling is an emotional act. The killer would rush his victim, even if she were sitting down. Any strangler would grab her neck and be pushing her back into the lab, chair and all. There would have to be a very passionate motivation, as well. Doesn't it strike you as peculiar that Tom would choke her smack in a doorway where he was bound to be seen? There's something too weird about that," I concluded.

"Peter," Dr. Gardner said, "your father told me you have plans to become a professional detective."

"Yes, sir." He had an expression on his face that broadcasted, "Jeez this kid is out of his mind." I made a little more small talk, then took the elevator down from Gardner's office. I caught up with Mackenzie in the planetarium's lower lobby as she and a couple of dozen others were being herded away from Hallway C.

"Let's get out of here," I said, grabbing her hand and pulling her toward a rear exit.

Outside, Mackenzie and I headed downtown on

Columbus Avenue past a sidewalk café and newsstands with tabloid newspaper headlines: "Doc Removes Wrong Head From Two-Headed Baby" and "Cannibal Chief Eats Mail-Order Brides." The usual evening rush-hour crowd flowed past us. Old men in yarmulkes. Women Rollerblading and pushing along on trendy aluminum scooters. Delivery boys from Zabar's and Fairway Market peddled like lunatics on their bikes to get people's dinners to them.

As we walked, I told Mackenzie about Mirsky and Congers, and how they went at each other's throats. "Either one of them would have knocked off Farr in a New York minute, if you ask me," I said. "But Gardner not only thinks Tom's the murderer, he thinks he's a druggie and a crook."

"What did you tell him?"

"I told him I think there's something preposterous about his scenario, including Tom's hands around Conchetta's throat. It sounds so . . . staged."

"I don't think we'll get any further until we talk to Tom and get his side of the story," Mackenzie said. "I mean, the eyewitness reports are damning."

"Can your mom set up a visit with Tom in jail?" I asked. "He's probably down at the holding station on Centre Street."

"One phone call will do it, I bet. Mom's poker group just took in another city councilman and an assistant D.A."

"Nice." Mrs. Riggs is one of the most social and net-worked coroners I know. I think she's got enough connections in the right places to get just about anything done around New York City that she wants.

Mackenzie and I have only been slightly involved in one other murder case—the one Mirsky mentioned. That was when a window dresser was killed when he was putting in a new display one night at Bloomingdale's. For three days thousands of people walked by Bloomie's and didn't think there was anything strange about his body in the window with all the mannequins; but it took me and Mackenzie only one look, and we knew it was a corpse.

The main reason we're interested in baffling and dangerous cases is because we're nosy. I'm the worst, but I can't help noticing when anything is odd. I'm basically a better judge of straight facts than Mackenzie. She's better at psychoanalytical and psychic stuff, a talent that she inherited from her father. She gets these intense chills on the top of her head whenever she senses something isn't quite right. She's better at the riddles of being human, figuring out why people do what they do. I'm more like the left brain to her right lobes.

"You want to stop over for dinner tonight?" Mackenzie asked. "Mom's making her homemade pizza."

"You said she was doing autopsies all day?"

"Yes . . ."

"Then it's a pass."

Mackenzie stopped short and put her hands on her hips. "Hey, my mom washes her hands before she kneads the dough, you know. Is that what you're getting at?"

"Of course not," I said, laughing. I gave her a little slap on the back like I had been only kidding, but I wasn't.

I walked Mackenzie right to the front door of her family's brownstone on West 70th Street. We had a little discussion about whether the rising moon was a gibbous or not a gibbous, said good night, and I turned and started away. "Ten o'clock at the subway tomorrow," I called over my shoulder as I broke into a jog. I ran all the way down to where I live in Lincoln Plaza, which is on Broadway at 63rd Street. My father and I live on the sixteenth floor, in a two-bedroom with a sunken living room, cheapo parquet floors, and a view of the Chagall murals in the lobby at Lincoln Center Opera House across the street.

I wasn't inside my apartment for more than five minutes before my aunt Doris hurtled herself through the door carrying a couple of loaded shopping bags. She and my uncle John, a photographer for *National Geographic*, live in 21C—five stories above.

"Kiss kiss," she said to me and headed straight for the kitchen. She does all the food shopping and makes certain

I have a good dinner every night whenever my dad's away.

She set the table, her chatter like machine-gun fire. "I didn't like the veal today, so you got roast chicken and a portion of Caesar salad with extra anchovies. The cannolis were just okay, so you ended up with Cherry Garcia, red globe grapes, and a cantaloupe." She had a rhythm to her speech that sometimes made her sound as though she were speaking in pentameter.

"Thanks, Aunt Doris," I said. By the time I finished washing up, the chicken and vegetables had been zapped in the microwave and were waiting for me.

"Your uncle's been driving me crazy since he got back from Australia," Aunt Doris said while I chewed on a chicken thigh. "He does nothing but sort and crop his slides."

"He must have gotten some good shots," I said. I waited uneasily for the inevitable. I don't know why it is, but I noticed that whenever there's food being served and eaten, Aunt Doris always gets around to mentioning some absolutely unsavory thing that would make anyone with a sensitive stomach toss their cookies. I knew it was coming.

"Did you know that the kangaroo and the emu are represented on Australia's coat of arms? Well, I didn't. I was absolutely staggered to find out that the Aussies are the only ones on earth who actually cook and devour their national symbols," Aunt Doris said.

"Isn't that the most bizarre thing you've ever heard?"

If only I had known then what I know now about Case #1, I could have told Aunt Doris a thing or two about bizarre.

4

Tombs and Duck Sauce

**The next morning Mackenzie and I met** at Columbus Circle and grabbed the subway downtown to the "Tombs," as the Manhattan jail is better known by experienced cops and crooks. "I didn't know how to dress for the Tombs," Mackenzie muttered groggily. "You always hear about jail guys hollering and banging their metal cups on the bars. I didn't want to set anyone off. Blue jeans. Yellow blouse. What do you think?"

"Hannibal Lecter would love it," I said.

She was not amused. "I tried to call Dad in Oslo last night to ask him about Tom, but I never got hold of him. The time was all mixed up, and he was scheduled to present a paper entitled 'Why Freud Fainted While Passing His Father's Graveyard.' I'll try him again this afternoon."

We came up out of the subway at the junction of Police Plaza and the Avenue of the Finest. The curbs were lined with dozens of parked NYPD and Traffic Control vans and cars. There were groups of uniformed cops and office workers at the coffee and bagel stands.

The Manhattan jail was across the street, its windowless walls of bright-orange brick making it look more like a modern elementary school than a tank to hold criminals.

"Can you imagine how terrible Tom must feel?" Mackenzie said. "You always see and hear on TV and in the movies about all those jails with rats and soup bowls with a single egg floating in it like an eyeball. And all those violent things guards and inmates do."

"That's more of what goes on after criminals have been convicted and sent to a prison. Our prison system sucks, big-time. When they're in a holding tank at the local jail, it's not as bad," I said. "But Tom's got to be very frightened."

A Metro Care ambulance sped by with its siren screaming as Mackenzie and I went in the front door. The reception guard made us pass through a metal detector. He frisked me. A policewoman popped out of an alcove like a figure from a Swiss cuckoo clock to frisk Mackenzie.

"We're here to see Tom Boggs," I said.

One of the policemen, who looked like a professional wrestler on heavy steroids, had us sign in. They made us clip on small plastic passes and led the way down a long corridor past several offices. At the end, a tall guard opened a metal door with a small bulletproof window. The muscular one unlocked yet another door and led Mackenzie and me into a vast rectangular, caged room.

There was a long steel table with a half dozen heavy wood chairs around it.

"They'll bring him out," the brawny cop said. He indicated for Mackenzie and me to sit at the table. "You get five minutes with the perpetrator." He pulled up a chair at the far end of the room in a glass cubicle, giving us at least a little privacy.

My first sight of Tom was that of a thin, tall, and limping silhouette coming down the hallway toward our gated room. The morning sun blasted through a set of barred windows behind him. A lone Hispanic guard with a ponytail held him by his right arm, helping him move forward in small, pathetic steps. His hands were cuffed behind his back.

The sight of Tom somehow made me remember how I hadn't really done all for him I might have since he'd come into our lives. And I thought of a note Mackenzie had e-mailed to me when she and I were first getting to know each other. It was part of a quote by George Eliot on the subject of friendship: "Oh, the comfort of having neither to weigh thoughts nor measure words, but to pour them all out just as they are, knowing that a faithful hand will keep what is worth keeping, and then, with the breath of kindness, blow the rest away."

"Well, I guess if we're going to be real friends to Tom on this case, we're going to have to be toothpaste," I said.

Mackenzie looked at me like I was insane.

"Ready to squeeze through some tight places," I explained.

The guard opened the gated doorway and brought Tom in to sit at the table. He unlocked one of the cuffs, then relocked it so the chain passed through a thick metal ring attached to the table.

"Tom," Mackenzie said, as she and I moved down to the chairs closest to him.

"I'm sorry," Tom said. His eyes were red, his hands shaking. He was hardly recognizable, with his face gaunt, exaggerating his slightly bucked teeth. He tossed his head aristocratically, almost with bravado, but he looked on the verge of tears. A single silver loop was in his left ear. He had been allowed to keep a small cross on a gold chain around his neck.

"What happened?" I asked.

Tom squirmed in his chair. It took him a long while to find his voice. His jaw trembled. "I don't know."

Mackenzie and I looked at each other. I turned my glance back at Tom, studying him closely. "How can you *not* know?"

Tom furrowed his brow. It appeared as if it were painful just to try to think. "They say I killed Dr. Farr," Tom said. "I couldn't have. I just know I couldn't have. . . ." His voice trailed off.

"Witnesses saw you with your hands around her throat, Tom," Mackenzie said gently.

Tom began to cough. One of the guards brought him

a paper cup of water. "I don't remember anything from . . ." I watched Tom straining to remember. ". . . from the time I was sweeping the hallway . . . I remember I had the broom. Then, the next thing I was looking into Dr. Farr's face. Into her eyes. They were like glass. Frozen. Max was taking my hands away from her throat. I don't understand how I could have hurt her. Killed her. What would make me do something like that?"

"That's what we want to find out," I said.

"Who's feeding Aristotle?" Tom asked. "Who's taking care of her bugs? She loved them. I miss Aristotle. Blondie, the biggest one. All the tarantulas and . . ." His voice broke off.

"We'll make sure someone's giving them water and food," Mackenzie said. "Don't worry about that."

"Dr. Farr was a great lady. She was kind to me," Tom said, barely able to speak. "She'd give me half of a sandwich. She'd asked how I was doing . . . like a mother. . . ."

Suddenly, there was a scream. "You get away from him! Get away! Leave him alone!"

Mackenzie and I turned around to see a guard trying to restrain a rail of a woman with a face that was wrinkled like a dried apple. We recognized Tom's mother, had seen her come to meet Tom at the museum for lunch from time to time. She would bring brown bags of sandwiches and bottles of Gatorade or Pepsi. "You talk to his lawyer, that's who you talk to!" Mrs. Boggs was shouting as she charged forward.

The wrestler guard came quickly over. "You're going to have to leave," he told Mackenzie and me.

Mrs. Boggs was in our faces now, still yelling at us. "You're making trouble for him, that's what you're doing. He wouldn't be here if you and your father hadn't meddled," she hurled at Mackenzie. She turned her snarl to me. "You couldn't leave us alone. I never wanted him to work at the museum anyway. You do-gooders! You lousy do-gooders!"

"We're sorry, Mrs. Boggs," I said. For a moment I heard echoes of my mother's own voice—the urgency and strength with which she defended me on the streets of New York. When my mom was alive she had always stood up for me, even if I was wrong. She'd tell me exactly *how* I was wrong later, but, in any moment of danger from a crazed taxi driver or lunatic on the streets, she was a lioness. I could see the same instinct in Mrs. Boggs's eyes.

"We were only trying to help Tom and you," Mackenzie added over her shoulder as she and I were led out of the cage and moved down the hall toward the exit.

"I didn't kill her. I know I didn't. I know I didn't kill her," Tom cried out. His voice reverberated off the brick walls, like a shriek in a school gymnasium.

I shook my head as Mackenzie and I broke back out into the sunshine of the plaza.

"Oh, God," Mackenzie said. "His mother is a screwball."

"At least one bubble off plumb," I said, "but she's only protecting Tom. She makes peanuts washing floors at the World Trade Center, and Tom used to help her pay the rent. She must be desperate. She does look like the steamroller of life has driven over her a few times, but what mother wouldn't freak out if her son were arrested for knocking off somebody?"

"She could be psychotic, you know," Mackenzie said. "And so could Tom. It could be something genetic. I can't believe that was the same timid woman we met a year ago. She was grateful to my dad for treating Tom. Thankful he got a job at the museum. Now she's bonkers."

"I don't know about that," I said, as we headed north toward Chatham Square and Mott Street.

"Where are we going, by the way?" Mackenzie asked.

"Chinatown. It's lunchtime. My treat."

"When you put it that way . . ."

"And after lunch, we need to go to the morgue. I think we could use a little chat with your mom. It'd be routine for them to test Tom's blood for drugs, and she might have some data on Dr. Farr's autopsy."

"Oh, P.C.," Mackenzie said, stopping suddenly in a patch of sunshine. "Tom didn't kill anyone. I know it."

"Chills on the top of your head?"

"Big-time."

# 5

## Life at the Morgue

**It was only a few blocks** from Police Plaza to the heart of Chinatown. I picked up the pace on Mott Street past open markets with buckets of blue crabs and live rock bass squirming in shallow water. Shoppers were selecting fresh pea pods, chicken feet, weird cabbages, and hanging roasted ducks that had twisted barbecued heads. I don't know about you, but I think we ought to have an American Society for the Prevention of Cruelty to Fowl, Fish, and Crustaceans. Also, maybe laws against making chocolate-covered ants and sautéing snails in garlic butter, too.

"My dad's favorite place down here is the Nom Wah Tea Parlor," Mackenzie said. "He has a theory that a daily dosage of shrimp and lobster sauce is one of the best ways to cure mood swings."

"Your dad has a lot of interesting theories," I said, turning into the doorway of Dim Sum Palace. We sat at a table near the front window that looked out onto a horde of shoppers. The Chinese waitresses began to push their carts of bacon-wrapped shrimp, custard tarts, and plump sugar-coated meat puffs our way as

Mackenzie called her mom on her cell phone. We arranged to see her after lunch at the morgue and forensics laboratories compound on Worth Street.

"What do you *really* think about the case?" I asked.

Mackenzie knew I wasn't talking about the food. "Tom acted like he was in shock. I mean, he was out of it. Too far out of it to lie, I think. But the bottom line is—he had no motive, and a lot of other people at the museum did."

"I believe he *thinks* he didn't kill her." I took another little dish of shrimp off the dim sum cart. "At least, I think he actually doesn't remember killing her. So I ask myself, 'What kind of a person wouldn't remember strangling someone? What sort of person in what kind of condition?'"

"Someone who was in shock, traumatized," Mackenzie said, munching on a mouthful of water chestnuts. "Or—maybe even hypnotized."

"Bingo."

"But people don't do anything really vicious under hypnosis that they wouldn't ordinarily do."

"Not necessarily so. There have been cases where people have murdered someone without knowing that's what they were doing. I read how a woman in Albany was hypnotized to kill her father by programming her so that every time he praised her cooking, she put salt on his food—when it was really strychnine in the salt shaker."

"Oh, yeah. I remember reading about that case," Mackenzie said. "But I think it was *cyanide*."

"Same difference," I said. "But choking someone would be a horse of a different color."

Mackenzie yanked off her sunglasses so she could really see my eyes. "So, do you think Tom was hypnotized or not?"

"Maybe yes, maybe no. Ever since World War II, the military has come up with techniques that go far beyond hocus-pocus. Ways to wear someone down. To deprive them of sleep and food, and warp their minds. Tom might have been brainwashed. I read there were chemicals that can do the same thing to you. Drugs that only some specially educated people would know about. People like professors and archaeologists and . . ."

"People who work at a museum," Mackenzie said. "The kind of people who may have wanted Dr. Farr dead."

"That's why we're getting out of here now," I said, wiping my mouth with a paper napkin and calling for the check.

Once outside on Chatham Square, Mackenzie took out her cell phone and called her mom to see if she could test for any really weird stuff in Tom's blood. We headed back downtown past the Department of Motor Vehicles and the U.S. Court. When we arrived at the morgue, an assistant brought us down to the head coroner's office. Mackenzie and I had to wait a few minutes while Mrs. Riggs finished dictating the final details of an autopsy report on a homeless woman found on West 43rd Street three nights earlier.

"How many bodies do you usually have around here?" I asked while Mrs. Riggs was washing up at a sink in her office. Mackenzie had gone to the ladies room in the hall.

"Over sixty-three chillin' in there now, P.C.," Mrs. Riggs said. She moved gracefully, placing stainless steel instruments, scalpels, and bone vises into an autoclave for sterilization. "We're usually good for ten to twenty cadavers a day. We've got larger facilities at several locations around the city for major disasters. Plane crashes. Crowd stampedes at rock concerts or explosions at the World Trade Center. Things like that. We never know what's going to happen around this town."

"What percentage of the corpses that you bring in are those of people who have been murdered?"

"I'd say about half. Most people think the majority are slaughtered by exotic maniacs with knives and guns or hammers. It *ain't* so. Most victims are knocked off by their jealous husbands or greedy wives or kids—nuts from their own families. It's usually over money or some uncle fooling around somewhere where he shouldn't be."

"That's horrible," I said. "It sounds like it's 'Home Sweet Homicide.'"

"Bingo," Mrs. Riggs said.

Mrs. Riggs discouraged people from calling her "Doctor" and preferred "Mrs. Riggs" or just "Kim." She was in her was mid-forties, tall, with exceptionally broad shoulders and prematurely gray hair as long as her daughter's. "Confidentially, I'll tell you that we've finished Dr. Farr's autopsy. Nothing unusual there. And the lab has already run its routine drug tests on a sample of Tom's blood. It was negative for weed, coke, and alcohol. As you know, that's all they usually test for when they bring in a suspect who looks whacked out. After Mackenzie's call, I had my secretary, Rio, bring over the rest of the sample so we can run it on a chromatograph to check for other substances."

The autoclave began to steam. It looked like a silver pressure cooker the size of a bathtub. Through the view window of the office, I could see an assistant coroner was examining parts of a body on one of the roll-out slabs in the refrigeration room.

Mrs. Riggs adjusted an old fedora. The hat, which she wore constantly, had belonged to her father. There were a couple of purple and red fishing flies in its tattered band. Her father, Rubert Rolitzek, when he was alive, was the most famous head coroner New York City had ever had. A book he wrote called *When Death Delights* was on *The New York Times* best-seller list for thirty-one weeks. I read it a half dozen times. It was about how Dr. Robitzek had matched the precise identities and body parts of over a hundred and eighty victims of a midair plane collision over Brooklyn working only from things like blood types and dental records. His book is my forensics bible.

Mackenzie came back and Mrs. Riggs led the way down the hall to another lab. The room's double-height shelves were filled with everything from bottles of chemicals and a vault for acids to models of the atom and human organs floating in formaldehyde. The center of the room was a long black granite island with several sinks, copper faucets, and clusters of gas jets that looked like stainless steel hands. I noticed a large electron spectroscope sitting squat at the end of the room like a robot. An old Chinese man in a white lab coat stood at attention.

"This is Dr. Chin," Mrs. Riggs said to Mackenzie and me. "He's a veteran in forensic and analytical chemistry. Probably the top analytical spectroscopy authority in the country."

Dr. Chin smiled during the greetings. When the small talk was over, he turned to face a three-foot vertical glass column that was filled with specialized chemical gel layers and treated paper strips. At a nod from Mrs. Riggs, he poured a flask of liquid into the very top of the column.

"He's added solvents and boosters to the sample of Tom's blood," Mrs. Riggs explained. "The various parts of the blood will be absorbed at different levels of the gel and paper stripping. It sort of fingerprints everything that's in the blood."

Mrs. Riggs pointed to the top of the chromatograph. Distinct layers had already begun to form. "What's showing now are the usual components of blood. Water, hemoglobin, iron content." She lowered her finger slowly down the outside of the cylinder. "Plasma components . . . nitrogen compounds, fats . . . all the common separation and layering we see when we run blood . . ."

I noticed Mrs. Riggs tense. She moved closer to the column, and adjusted her granny glasses.

"What it is?" I asked.

"I'm not sure . . ."

"What?" Mackenzie wanted to know.

"We have to let the drip finish," Mrs. Riggs said, "but there is something Dr. Chin will have to look at under the electron spectroscope."

When the chromatography was finished, Dr. Chin lay the cylinder down on the lab table and pushed out the gel plug. He took a sample of the layer Mrs. Riggs had indicated, placed it onto a slide, and slid it into the specimen holder of the large spectroscope. Dr. Chin sat in front of the spectroscope's console and fine-tuned it so the light passing through the chemical sample would be precisely identified. He pressed the printer button to get a record of the identification. Dr. Chin passed the slip of paper to Dr. Riggs.

"Did Tom have a heart condition?" Mrs. Riggs asked.

"My husband didn't mention one. Did he take heart medicine of any kind?"

I looked to Mackenzie.

"No," Mackenzie said. "Dad had me help Tom fill his prescriptions."

"What did you find?" I asked Mrs. Riggs.

"There's a very powerful adrenoceptor in Tom's blood," Mrs. Riggs said. "What you may have heard of as a beta-blocker."

"Yes . . ." I said.

"But this one is rare—and very specific. It's one of the most powerful class of drugs of its kind—and there was a high level of it in Tom's blood when the sample was taken. It's the kind of dosage one would only prescribe if a patient had a very serious heart problem, like a dissected aorta or a rupturing heart wall."

"Would this particular adrenoceptor make Tom more aggressive?" I said. "Could it have made him violent?"

Mrs. Riggs shook her head. "No," she said. "This one would mellow you out. It might explain his spaced-out appearance when he was brought in. When some adrenoceptors are not used for heart problems, they're sometimes called 'performance' drugs. Some actors and speakers are prescribed them to reduce anxiety and stage fright."

"Would it help condition Tom to be hypnotized?" Mackenzie asked. "Make it easier for someone to control his mind?"

"What a strange question to ask," Mrs. Riggs said. She had to mull that one over. Dr. Chin gave her a nod. "I never thought of it like that," she said, "but it could. The more relaxed a subject is, the easier it is to put him into a hypnotic state. But mind control would be a long shot in this case, kids, don't you think?"

"But not impossible," I said.

"No," Mrs. Riggs agreed. "Not impossible. I realize that you two feel something's wrong, but the police are still going to go with the sticky fact that witnesses found Tom's hands around Conchetta's throat. An unprescribed adrenoceptor in his blood isn't going to get him off the hook. It's possible he could have raided somebody's medicine cabinet."

"I don't think that's what happened," I said. Sure, I thought about the druggie Gardner had pointed out as one of Tom's new pals in the park. Mackenzie or I would have picked up on it if Tom were on drugs. "I think someone gave Tom this drug deliberately. Somehow, someway, somebody made Tom kill Dr. Farr—or made it look like he did."

"Oh, my." Mrs. Riggs thought a moment longer. "I don't know what to say except that, this feeling you have—this hunch—I think my father would have said, 'Follow it wherever it takes you.'"

"I *know* he would have," I said.

A bell was sounding on the autoclave. Mrs. Riggs

turned and started back down the hall. Mackenzie and I trailed after her. "Be careful on this one," she said, waving us back as she slowly opened the steaming cauldron. "Be very careful."

## 6

## Megabyting a Murderer

**By eight o'clock Saturday night** Mackenzie was able to call me with the precise identification of the chemical found in Tom's blood. A second refined spectroscopy showed that the adrenoceptor was an isomer of one called propranolol hydrochloride. What was most unusual was that it was contaminated with traces of a raw red dye.

"*Henna,*" Mackenzie said. "That's the name of the dye—one from Africa. They use it as an ingredient in various hair coloring preparations."

I sat at the desk in my room trapping the apartment's cordless phone receiver between my head and my shoulder. Both hands were free to type notes into my computer. "What does finding the traces of henna *mean?*"

"Dr. Chin said this particular adrenoceptor was most likely bought in Egypt or Morocco," Mackenzie said. "Henna is largely Egyptian grown, but most North African merchants carry it as well. Over there nearly every drug is available over the counter. You know, without prescription. Every hole-in-the-wall pharmacy shop sells stuff like codeine or penicillin, poisons, aphrodisiacs, you name it, like bags of Twizzlers. They all traditionally sell basic dyes as well. There would be henna in their shops side by side with the heavy-duty drugs, so there'd be traces of raw henna in practically anything they sold."

"That'll help us."

"That's what I thought. And my dad just called. It's morning in Oslo. He confirmed that the only drug he had prescribed for Tom was a low dosage of Zoloft, an antidepressant. He doesn't know where or why Tom would have gotten this form of propranolol hydrochloride. It's not the kind of drug anybody on the street's really interested in because it gives no great high or anything like that. He thought it was really weird." She took a deep breath.

"Did you ask your father anything about hypnosis?" I asked.

"Of course," Mackenzie said. "I knew you'd want me to. He gave it to me in a nutshell. He said hypnosis is hard to define. They used to call it 'sleep,' which was kind of weird and an understatement. It's been around since ancient times . . ."

"Religious ecstasies and trances," I said.

"Right—that sort of thing. Dad said at least one out of four people can be hypnotized. Drugs, the adrenoreceptor, shiny objects, all that stuff can help a subject go under a spell. A good subject can be hypnotized with or without their consent. . . ."

"So Tom may never have known anyone was doing anything to him."

"Dad told me a lot of freaky stuff like how whole TV audiences have been hypnotized by watching a hypnotist on television. You get eyelid closure. Make the subject get into a rhythm like their breathing. It doesn't much matter how that's done. Blind and deaf people can be hypnotized. Isn't that wild? And there's a technique some stage magicians use where they give you a chop on one side of your carotid sinus and it causes a momentary loss of consciousness. If they hit both carotid sinuses at the same time, you can die. And people who want to be *liked* make the best subjects."

"That's our Tom."

"Also, Spalding Kazinski has been calling every hour on the hour. He wants to know if the three of us can meet on Monday and get a look at the Ganesh necklace at the museum."

"There was a message from him on my answering machine when I got home. He is such a loser."

"Jeez, you're cynical tonight. We ought to give him a chance. At least he sounds enthusiastic, and, you know, it's an ill wind that doesn't blow somebody some good."

"That sounds like something my aunt Doris would say."

"She did."

"Look, give Jesus a call and bring him up to speed on

the propanolol and our hypnosis theory," I said. "Tell him we think this might be a slight case of murder by proxy. Tom was definitely set up. I'll check out the North African connection on the museum database. See what he can find out about anyone on the staff who ever fiddled with any kind of mind control or hypnosis. Voodoo. Tarot cards. Ouija boards. Anything really zany."

"Okay," Mackenzie agreed. "But I don't think Tarot cards are *that* zany."

"I stand corrected," I said. "I am also barely standing, because it's getting a little late and I'm tired."

"And cranky."

"You're right. I'm sorry. Next week I'll draw you out on tarot cards."

"Apology accepted," Mackenzie said. "By the way, I remembered one other freaky medical use of hypnosis my dad mentioned that I thought you should know about."

"What?" I asked.

"It's a way of getting at a person's subconscious. See, you hypnotize the person and tell them they're sitting in a dark movie theater and watching a movie in which they're *starring*."

"Then what?"

"Well, you let them watch the 'movie' awhile and see how their character is behaving, and then you tell them to walk around to the *back* of the screen and they'll be able to see what is making them act that way. And it works! My dad said it's one of the best ways of finding out the truth about anything." She went silent for a moment. "Just think how Tom must be feeling tonight going to bed locked up in that jail. The hard bed. Some pillow that smells of disinfectant or has mites in it."

"We've got to prove he's innocent and get him out of there," I said. "We've got to."

I hung the phone up in its cradle, went out to the kitchen, and poured myself a bowl of Frosted Mini-Wheats and a glass of milk. That's how I like to go to bed every night, with milk and a snack like cereal, pistachio nuts, or Cheez-Its. Aunt Doris had brought down a breaded slice of eggplant parmigiana, an artichoke stuffed with sun-dried tomatoes, and a pint of Death by Chocolate ice cream, but I felt like something crunchy. Plus, I hadn't been very hungry after she had told me that Hong Kong restaurants roast over a hundred thousand St. Bernard dogs every year and use their fur and skins to make bedroom slippers.

I ate my snack in bed and fiddled for a while with Resident Evil 3: Nemesis on my Play Station. I expected to be asleep before midnight, but there was too much new and important information to process. Half of the two hundred people who worked at the museum traveled at least a few months of the year. I figured at least a dozen of those had probably been to Egypt or Morocco in the last six months, even if it were just for a plane refueling or to make a connection through Casablanca or Cairo. I've traveled enough around the world with my dad to know there's a pharmacy even at the dinkiest commercial airports.

I knew my pal Jesus, computer whiz par excellence, would routinely check everything I came up with. As I closed my eyes, I decided to do my addition for the day so my mind could churn it over as I slept. I never forget the fact that a chemist discovered the cyclical structure for benzene by dreaming of a snake swallowing its own tail.

The sum to date: *Dr. Farr was choked to death. Tom had no motivation, but half the museum did. Whoever killed Conchetta somehow had managed to drug and frame Tom. The murderer is cruel. Slick. The killer thinks he's getting away with it.*

I began to replay the confrontation between Dr. Mirsky and Dr. Congers, and I knew that Mackenzie and I would have a few alibis to ask about and check out. Of course, the police wouldn't be the least interested in asking for alibis since they *knew* Tom was the murderer. In my last moments awake, I imagined a very large, glistening lizard. A Komodo dragon with the head of a ghastly human. A septic reptile prowling the stairways and corridors of the museum. Laughing. Smug.

But what the real killer of Dr. Farr didn't know was that when Mackenzie and I bite into something, we lock our teeth onto it and hang on like bulldogs.

## 7

## Exploring

**The next morning,** I decided to get up to the museum and find out where Congers, Mirsky, and anybody else who really hated Dr. Farr were at the time of the murder. Mackenzie called and said she and her mother were going to the early Sunday service at the Cathedral of St. John the Divine, and that she'd meet me at the museum as soon afterward as she could.

I walked uptown along the park. An elderly woman with frosted eyelids was walking her Egyptian greyhound, the only one of its breed I had ever seen in Manhattan. A man in a purple jumpsuit with a beard like Rasputin and a feather turban ran excitedly behind the horse-drawn carriages scooping up manure to sell to penthouses for their potted azaleas and ficus trees. As usual, several fearless rats were commuting back and forth across Central Park West from a trash bin near the Dakota to a hole in the ground at the edge of the park.

I crossed CPW near a bronze bust of the explorer Alexander von Humboldt and joined the morning horde of students and fall tourists heading up the stairs to the museum entrance. Inside, Max's muscular, brooding assistant, Patience Griffin, was standing at the doorway of the security office.

"Hey, Patience, what's happening?" I asked.

"It's still a madhouse," Patience said. "Detectives are peeling off the museum workers one by one to interview them and take more statements."

I knew it would be routine police procedure for the detectives to interview them and gather any information that could be used in Tom's trial to prove whether Farr's murder was premeditated or an act of insanity. The propranolol in Tom's blood obviously wouldn't mean a thing to the police, yet.

"And Gardner's got a bunch of the staff up in the Hall of Minerals rehearsing their bits for the museum gala," Patience went on. "Obviously, it's going to take more than a strangling to cancel a fund-raiser around here."

"Figures," I said.

"Hey, P.C.! Hey!" came a smarmy voice as though from a nightmare. I spun around to see Spalding Kazinski dashing through the crowd toward me.

"What?" I said.

The whole bottom half of Spalding's face suddenly became a huge, artificial smile. He had a regular-size body except for his head, which was long and angular like a horse's, and his hair looked like congealing wet wads of rusting cotton.

"I was hoping we could start our report on Ganesh,

and I thought maybe you could get us a sneak peek at that necklace," Spalding said. "You know, the new one from India that no one's seen. Maybe we could take a Polaroid of it. Would that be a cool prop or what?"

"No way," I said. "They'll keep that necklace in the vault until the gala. Nobody's seen it."

"Oh, come on. You could get your father to pull strings. Last term you had those great museum drawings of medieval armor and that hilarious photo of Mackenzie in an iron maiden. Miss Conlan always gives extra credit for stuff like that."

"My father's in Sumatra."

"So e-mail him to cash in a few chips around here."

"He's in the jungle with apes," I said. Spalding kept moving closer to me. I felt like slapping his face like it was a paddle ball. "Hey, I've already downloaded a mess of stuff on Ganesh," he said. "You and Mackenzie have got to do *something*."

"Yeah," I said. "I've got to go. The three of us can have a meeting Wednesday or Thursday during study period." I turned, waved to Mrs. Ebb at her ticket drop, and started down the hallway toward the museum's IMAX Theater.

"It's the murder, isn't it!" I heard Spalding calling after me. "I'll bet all you're interested in is the murder!"

I ducked out of his sight down a staircase to the lower level.

Downstairs the only remnant of the crime scene left

in Hallway C was a single wooden barricade and an X of yellow police tape across the door to Farr's laboratory, the doorway where Tom had been seen with his hands around her throat. It was weird enough that she was killed sitting down in her desk chair, but now it seemed to me even more unlikely that anyone would strangle someone in such an exposed place unless they really *wanted* to be caught.

My dad's office was farther down the long hallway. He had always trusted me with a key and had cleared it with Gardner and Max. Ever since Mom died he knew I really liked being able to hang in his office, especially when he was away. I'd stop by a few times after school each week and do research, and sometimes I'd just chill on weekends and enjoy being surrounded by my dad's books and diplomas and archaeological dig thingamajigs. One whole wall was a hanging collage of chisels, stiff and fine brushes, and odd-shaped picks. I think he knew my being there, surrounded by the reality of his smarts and the tools of his important work, gave me a feeling of security and, I think, it gave me a lot of *nerve*.

I unlocked the door, went in, and put on the lights. My mother had decorated dad's office when he'd first gone to work at the museum. There were no windows in this section of the lower level. She had hung a curtain covered in bright images of sea horses and exotic jellyfish on the far wall so it appeared there was a window behind it, like they do at some Motel 8's and in the el cheapo cabins below the water line on bargain Caribbean cruises. Behind the curtain was the ugly wall of cinder block. I could never come into the office and see the pretty curtain without thinking of my mom.

I sat down at my dad's iMac. It was in the middle of a desk cluttered with archaeological magazines, clipped abstracts, and souvenirs from places like Tahiti and Java. A bookcase crammed with Natural Science encyclopedias and stacks of *Scientific American* was against the wall. I turned on the computer and brought up the search engine for the museum database. It was complicated to access from computers outside the museum. Only Jesus had enough savvy for that. Jesus could hack his way into Los Alamos and the Pentagon, if it was necessary and if he thought for a minute the FBI wouldn't lock him up for twenty years.

I brought up the staff files, and typed in the words North Africa/Egypt/Morocco and clicked the mouse. After three searches I was able to establish that eighty-three members of the staff had been in that part of the world at one time or another. When I refined the search to include only the last six months, the number of museum employees who had worked or visited the area was *nine*. I searched again to see which of those scientists were out of the country on research or special projects at the time of Conchetta's murder. That left a list of six possible suspects, two of which were, not surprisingly, Dr. Jeffrey Mirsky and Beverly Congers. I could tell from their files that they were both travel freaks and that several of their trips a few years earlier had overlapped, suggesting they were once an item—which would also explain why they now fought like a cobra and a mongoose.

I shut off the iMac, locked up the office, and headed upstairs toward the Hall of Minerals. As I passed the police barricade I realized there was something else Mackenzie and I had to do. I called her on her cell phone.

"What?" she said, sounding really disturbed.

"What's the matter?" I asked.

"It's the middle of the Offering and I forgot to shut the ringer off," she whispered. She made a growling sound. "Six hundred people in pews are *staring* at me."

"Oh, sorry," I said. But I also didn't want to waste a call. "I need you to stop by my uncle John's and borrow his camcorder. Bring it with you when you come. Okay? It's important."

Mackenzie sounded like she was hyperventilating when she disconnected, but I knew she'd get the job done.

## 8

## Mummy Dearest

**About eighteen of the staff had shown up** in the Hall of Minerals and had sprinkled themselves around a dais in the center of the room. A catering crew from Restaurants Associates was rolling plywood circles with eight- and twelve-foot diameters into place and dropping them on the top of card tables to make enough seating room for at least a couple of hundred guests. They threw white tablecloths over the circles and launched into hanging mobiles of giant plastic crystals dripping with strands of paste diamonds and phony rubies. I took a seat on one of the rises next to the hall's moon rock collection.

I watched Lieutenant Helen Krakowski stroll in and out every ten minutes or so. Krakowski wore regulation blue police trousers and shirt over her squat figure, but sported a multicolored jacket that looked like it was made from a Guatemalan shawl. She had black hair cut like a china doll's. Two uniformed cops stood at the office doorway assisting her.

I recognized the one new face at the gala rehearsal,

Dr. Liam Spiegelman, an enormous man in a high-tech motorized wheelchair with all the bells and whistles. My pal Jesus is on home study and is wheelchair-bound, too, but he has the old-fashioned kind he has to push himself. He's lost a lot of muscle in his legs from multiple sclerosis, but he's got the strongest arms of anyone I know. Still, I couldn't help thinking it'd be cool if he could have a top-of-the-line powered chair like Spiegelman's.

I'd seen Dr. Spiegelman's face in the September museum newsletter my father had brought home. The newsletter had included a photo of Spiegelman flanked by Gardner and several of the other staff members, including my father, welcoming him to the museum. Spiegelman had been headhunted from a museum in Vancouver because of his expertise in Indian antiquities.

The sound of Mirsky laughing cut over every other noise in the room. Congers was off to one corner near a brightly lit collection of malachite and azurite in a display case. Her glances at Mirsky looked like flying daggers, and it didn't take long to figure out why.

"I'll be a lot fairer than Farr ever was," Mirsky was braying to the rehearsal gathering. He halted his giraffelike gait in front of Gardner. "You won't be sorry," Mirsky said. "I'll see that everyone at the museum gets a fair shake when it comes to the travel and research grants."

"I'm sure you will," Dr. Gardner said, not even

looking at Mirsky. "You did have the seniority for the position."

"I had that a long time ago," Mirsky said.

I waited to pick my shot to talk to Lieutenant Krakowski. It came when Gardner was telling everyone about the guest list and assigning one scientist to each table and Mirsky had launched shamelessly into the promotion of the public lecture he was scheduled to give that afternoon at the Ethical Culture School on the paleontology topic "Fossils Buried with Humans."

"Excuse me, Lieutenant," I whispered to her as she was watching Mirsky hold center stage. "I was wondering if Dr. Riggs notified you and the police yet about the adrenoreceptor they found in Tom Boggs's blood?"

Krakowski looked at me with the eyes of a ticked-off codfish. "Who *are* you?"

"P.C. Hawke," I said. "My father's the head of archaeology here at the museum."

"Well," she said, "how about you just sit down and wait until I'm ready to talk to you?"

"Sure," I said, "but I just wanted to make certain that you knew Tom Boggs was slipped a mind-altering drug. Somebody set Tom up."

"P.C., do you have a hearing problem?"

"No. It's just that there's a lot more to this case than meets the eye. There's someone else involved in this murder and you'd better start asking some of these people here today where they were at the time Dr. Farr was killed. I think Tom Boggs was hypnotized." I hadn't realized it, but I had raised my voice. Dr. Gardner and half the staff at the speaker's platform were staring at me.

A strange, low sound came from Lieutenant Krakowski, like a faint gurgling. "You know you've got a big mouth, kid," she said. "I want you to leave now, and if I were you, I'd stay out of police business. I know we've arrested the right guy, your buddy or not. The museum director thinks we have. The mayor thinks we have. And the police board that's going to vote on my overdue promotion next week knows we have. This case is going to the district attorney tomorrow morning, so we can let a judge and jury decide if he's guilty."

At that moment I felt like juicing half a grapefruit on her nose. She was so close to me I could see she had a slight mustache and that her ear hairs needed clipping. I moved still closer until my lips were practically touching her brow. "Look, ma'am, I don't mean to be rude, but this case is not closed. I'm just telling you that you should be calling Mrs. Riggs, checking the alibis of everyone who hated Dr. Farr, and . . ."

Lieutenant Krakowski turned toward the center platform and brayed to Gardner, "Get this guy out of here!"

Gardner headed toward me with a frown. Several more of the staff were really staring now. "I'm going," I called to Gardner. I spun on my heels and took off toward the rear exit. If I stayed any longer, I knew I would have said a lot more I'd be sorry for, and as it was, I knew I had probably been overheard saying too much. I took a staircase up a flight to a staff shortcut above the Hall of Human Biology and Evolution. I knew I'd better get back to my dad's office and stay there until Mackenzie arrived. She'd know where to find me.

The passageway snaked behind and through the closed Halls of Mexico and Central America and the Birds of the World. The electricity had been turned off in these sections to allow for additional power lines to be brought up to the construction on the fourth floor. There was a series of stained-glass windows that cast rainbow shadows of angels and intricate rosettes on the walls.

Beyond was one of the most popular dioramas, one that showed how many cockroaches would populate a kitchen if a single pair were allowed to breed for a month and if all the offspring lived. It consisted of a mock-up kitchen with millions and millions of big roaches pinned to the walls and ceilings. It was difficult to see even the stove or refrigerator. A single glance at the display gave me the shivers. There were only two insects in the world that curdled my blood: cockroaches and scorpions. Most of the other bugs I sort of liked.

There was a sound behind me now, like a heat expansion in the hardwood floors. I tried not to think anything really paranoid, like that the real killer of Dr. Farr could well have been in the Hall of Minerals and had seen and heard my little chat with Lieutenant Krakowski. Tom's innocent. Oh, yes, someone *else* murdered Dr. Farr. . . .

Another sound.

I turned quicker this time, and saw a shadow far behind me. It seemed to move out of an alcove and disappear into a walkway behind a pile of construction Sheetrock and cables. There came a voice in the back of my mind. It was telling me something was wrong.

Every twenty feet now there were shafts of sunlight cutting in from side windows to illuminate rows of grinning masks, toothed shark heads, and condors with open, hooked beaks. I reached the stairway at the end of Birds of the World and started back down the two flights to the lower level. There came another sound.

Closer.

Someone following.

A chill deadened my legs. My instincts kicked in and I began to run down the stairs two at a time. The sound came again from the top. Footsteps echoing, descending the stairs in the darkness behind me. I broke out of the stairwell at the far end of Hallway C. Dim. Naked lightbulbs hung along the ceiling as I rushed past the barricade and yellow police tape on the door to Dr. Farr's laboratory. The next door down the hall, the door to Dr. Farr's office, was, oddly, open.

I stopped at the doorway.

"Hello," I called out, my voice cracking.

All sounds stopped. A narrow strip of light from the hall cast my shadow across the office area and loftlike room. I saw Conchetta's desk and file cabinets and computers standing like dead sentinels. Beyond the low bookcases that served as a room divider was the vast expanse of the lab and crime scene. The police should have taped and barricaded the office door, too, but they hadn't. What did they care? They had their killer.

There were faint rustlings from the stacks of cages and terrariums. The shadowy forms of tarantulas and Bombay wolf spiders the size of my hands crawled over beds of shredded newspapers and leaves. A row of three tall narrow metal cabinets caught my eye. They were the kind in which Conchetta would have hung her coat or kept umbrellas and lecture charts. Next to them was a large, olive-colored photocopier. I figured the police had probably at least done a cursory search, if not gone over every square inch of Conchetta's office, but I lifted the cover of the copier anyway.

A faded, old newspaper article lay on the glass beneath. I looked it over. The article was about a school bus accident in Galveston over thirty years ago. I checked the article and its photo for any familiar names, but there were none. I decided to fold it up, and tucked it into my pocket. If nothing else, I figured the article was one of the last things Conchetta had copied on her machine, and maybe there was a reason why.

I turned to leave, but the cabinets drew me to them. I

decided to open one of the metal doors. It had a rain-coat, what looked like a crochet-beaded sweater, and several reams of copy paper piled on top of each other. The second metal cabinet had a slide projector, projection screen, and cardboard boxes of books and lab supplies. I opened the third cabinet door.

There was a shriek.

A figure with the head of a mummy leaped out, causing the metal door to whack like a gunshot against the wall. I heard myself screaming now, as a wrinkled form charged at me. My hand flew up and caught a bony hand. The shrieking figure tried to flee past.

Suddenly the lights in the room were flicked on.

"Hold it," Mackenzie's voice cut over the racket. "Hold it right there."

Mackenzie stood at the doorway with her hand still on the light switch. Caught, the shape slowly raised itself to its full height. It was a woman clutching a white Yankee baseball cap.

"Mrs. Boggs!" I said, shocked.

Mrs. Boggs shook the hat at us. Her cracked lips opened. "It's my son's hat," she said, trembling. "I needed to get his hat. Tom left it. But he didn't kill anyone. He didn't." She pushed by us out the door and fled down the hallway.

Mackenzie stared at me. "My God, P.C., it's exciting, but I think we've really got to stop meeting like this."

## Hexes, Lies, and Videotape

**"That's one weird mother,"** I said, as I grabbed my uncle's camcorder out of Mackenzie's hand. She obviously didn't want the police to find any more incriminating evidence. Tom must have told her he'd lost his hat and she knew where it would be. You know how conscientious mothers can be." The words were no sooner out of Mackenzie's mouth when I could tell she was sorry she'd said them.

"Oh, sure," I said, wanting to let her know it was okay. "She's so out of it she must have figured her son leaving his Yankee cap was going to be the straw that broke the camel's back, the camel being three witnesses seeing him play Let's Choke Conchetta. I think Mrs. Boggs needs a set of shock treatments and a megadose of lithium."

"I guess she did overreact. What if it *is* a case of like mother, like son?" Mackenzie said. "You know, half of Tom could be nice and cool and the other half has this slight urge to strangle people."

I noticed Mackenzie looked extra tall. She saw me look down at her six-inch heels.

"Oh, yeah," Mackenzie said about her shoes. "They were on sale at Betsey Johnson. Day-Glo fake snake-skin."

"Perfect for sleuthing," I said.

"That's what I thought." She straightened the stretch of fringe on her leopard bag. "On the way in I saw Congers and asked her where she was when Farr bit the dust."

"What'd she say?"

"She said she was buying lemon-chicken and olives at Zabar's delicatessen, along with sixty thousand other people snagging lunch. Then I asked her if anyone was with her, and she said it was none of my business."

"Well, it's something . . ."

"Why'd you want the camcorder?"

"I want us to re-create the crime, and then we'll play the video back to Tom—like that hypnosis technique, make him feel like he's starring in his own movie. It could bring back his memory of the murder." I glanced at my watch. "It's just past two-thirty," I said. "We have to start taping *now*."

"Where?"

"This way."

We left Farr's office and headed down Hallway C to the planetarium lobby. As we walked, I quickly brought Mackenzie up to speed on everything and everyone I saw at the rehearsal, including my run-in with the crabby Helen Krakowski.

"Gardner gave Farr's job to Mirsky?" Mackenzie said.

"Yep," I said.

"Congers must be furious."

"She looked like she wanted to tear Mirsky's head off."

"When is the gala?"

"Tuesday night. You reminded me of something. Do you know the main reason people murder someone?"

"No."

"The main reason is greed," I said. "I wonder if anyone has stopped to think that Dr. Farr's murder might very well have something to do with the Ganesh necklace that they're unveiling at the gala. In terms of both its craftsmanship and the jewels themselves, it's literally priceless."

"Oh," Mackenzie said. "You think this might be one of those cases that where there's diamonds there's death?"

"Well, it seems to me there has to be some connection between the museum about to mount a display of priceless gems and the head of research biting the dust a few days before."

"You're right. It stinks."

"Like Gorgonzola."

We sat on a marble bench in the lobby for a few minutes while she skimmed over the results of my database search. I rattled off all the other details, like about how

Mirsky was giving a talk at Ethical Culture that night and how it wouldn't hurt if we caught it. A bigmouth like him could slip and say anything anywhere. Besides, we can corner him afterward and find out exactly where he was at the time of the murder.

At exactly two-forty, I opened a custodian's closet near the elevators, grabbed a pole with a yard-wide dust broom attached to it, and thrust it into Mackenzie's hands.

"What am I supposed to do?" Mackenzie said.

"Sweep."

"I know that part. *Where*?"

"Start here in the lobby," I said, turning on the camcorder and getting her image on its flip-up viewer screen. The camera had a zoom and automatic focus. "Pretend you're Tom and you're making the floor spiffy."

Mackenzie made a grimace as she began to sweep. We could hear the first of the symphonic bursts of music and explosions spilling out from behind the closed doors of the planetarium's auditorium. I had seen the Death of the Universe show several times during the year and knew the music was basically Rachmaninoff and one of those rip-off tribute songs to the memory of Princess Di.

"How *long* do I sweep?"

I glanced at my watch. "The first show is ending now like it did on Friday, and you're out here being very custodial and minding your own business and sweeping. Get going."

A group of nuns in a tour group walked through the lobby and stared at Mackenzie sweeping in her towering, loud shoes.

"I really feel idiotic," Mackenzie said. "Why don't *you* sweep and I'll do the camera work?"

I didn't answer because I was listening intently for the music from the show to reach its climax. I let the camcorder drink in all the images of the lobby. Everything Tom would have seen before the murder. The tiled walls and doors and signs to the Food Court. A few minutes later, the show ended and the audience started pouring out. I glanced back down at my watch. "Okay," I told Mackenzie. "Put the broom down."

"Where?"

"Anywhere."

Mackenzie groaned as she tossed the broom back in the closet. "Now what?"

"Walk slowly to Hallway C like you're confused or in a trance."

"Oh, nice."

She staggered off, and I followed her, videotaping her every move. I let the camera drift left and right to catch every sight along the way. The glistening white-and-aqua marble floor. A lighted meteorite on thick, shining steel pilings. A massive sculpture shaped like a hovering betatron.

Mackenzie turned down Hallway C.

"Way to go," I said. I kept the camera following her, letting it videotape each tile and sconce and strip of molding. "They said Tom went directly to the lab," I reminded her.

Mackenzie stopped at the barricaded and taped door of Farr's laboratory.

"Good," I said. "Hold it there a minute." I shot a close-up on the entire archway. "This is where he was seen choking her in the doorway." After a minute, I motioned her to move on. "Move down to Farr's office door like you did when you got here today."

Mackenzie stopped outside the office. I signaled her to go in. She opened the office door and flicked on the lights just as she had done when Mrs. Boggs had popped out of the closet. Inside, she walked to Conchetta's desk and stopped. I moved past her and let the camera focus on the racks of insects and lab tables at the far end of the big, long room. I pressed the zoom on the camera to get extra-close shots of the tarantula cages and a side shelf of terrariums filled with scorpions and other imported bugs.

Mackenzie saw a small refrigerator in the corner. She opened it and grabbed a can of Diet Pepsi that was sitting among the cartons of living food worms and containers of larvae. She flicked open the top and took a swig of the soda. "So we're going to show this tape to Tom, right?" she said, wiping her mouth. "You hope the video will trigger something. Make him remember how his hands ended up around her throat?"

I made a grunting sound that she knew was a *yes*.

Mackenzie let out a sigh. "Jail again."

"Yep."

She set her soda down on Conchetta's desk and started to look through the piles of notes and papers strewn across the top of it. Several large books on spiders and insects of the rain forests were piled high at one end of the desk. There was a stuffed in/out box for mail, a commercial-size stapler, a bottle of Wite-Out, and a holder in the shape of a pig filled with Ticonderoga #2 pencils.

A strange whirring sound and a large shadow intruded from the doorway. Mackenzie jumped at the sight of Liam Spiegelman in his motorized wheelchair.

"Oh, I didn't mean to startle you," Spiegelman said.

Mackenzie opened her mouth, but looked to me.

Spiegelman shifted a gear and propelled his wheelchair into the office. "What is this?" he asked. He glanced beyond a pile of boxes and an island sink to see the full length and inventory of the room. "I saw the police tape on the other door. Was this Dr. Farr's lab and office?"

"Yes," I said, turning the camcorder off.

Spiegelman stared at the stacks of small wire cages and glass terrariums. He moved closer. "My God, those are tarantulas! I had heard Dr. Farr's specialty was insects, but I didn't know she had a living collection down here." Several black Indian centipedes were crawling up the sides of the largest habitat. "I'm surprised the police didn't tape her office off along with her lab."

"We were surprised about that, too," Mackenzie said. "I guess they weren't too interested."

Close-up, I could see Spiegelman's wheelchair was as equipped and probably cost as much as a Subaru. His body looked too large for the chair, squished into it like a full-grown man in a school-bus seat. He squirmed to make himself comfortable and had that look people have when they're about to introduce themselves.

"We know who you are, Dr. Spiegelman," I said. "We've seen your picture in the newsletter. I'm P.C. My dad is Stephen Hawke, head of archaeology."

"Oh, yes," Spiegelman said, smiling. "Your dad was part of my welcoming committee. I remember we had chatted briefly over coffee. He was going off to do something with apes, wasn't he?"

"Orangutans," I said.

"I'm Mackenzie," Mackenzie said.

Spiegelman smiled broadly again, which got on my nerves. His features seemed too puffed and round and smooth and phony, like they were ready to roll off his face.

"This murder is a terrible thing," Spiegelman said. "It's so difficult to believe that nice custodian boy killed anyone. Tom was a great help to me."

"I remember he said you were setting up the displays for the gala," I said. "He was always helping a lot of the scientists do one thing or another."

"Yes. I was able to handle the smaller pieces, the major diamonds and rubies. Tom and a few of the others on the custodial staff helped reposition the larger meteorites and moon rocks. That sort of thing. It was Dr. Gardner's brainchild to have the gala dinner in the Hall of Minerals this year."

"It was a great idea," Mackenzie said.

"He tells me it's the hottest ticket in town." Spiegelman stared at the camcorder in my hand. "You're taping something?"

"Tom is a friend of ours," I said.

"Yes," Mackenzie seconded.

Spiegelman appeared to mull that over a moment. "I see," he said. "And you think videotaping the murder scene is going to . . . well, actually, I'm not sure exactly why you're videotaping Dr. Farr's laboratory."

"We think Tom was hypnotized," I said, watching carefully for Spiegelman's reaction. "That he was drugged *and* hypnotized."

"Oh, my," Dr. Spiegelman said. "What a frightening theory."

"It's more than theory," I said.

"Is it?" He pressed the steering stick of his wheelchair to the left. There was the whirring sound, and the

71

electric motor propelled the chair clockwise in a half circle. He glanced over Dr. Farr's bulletin boards on the walls. "I had no idea Farr's office was like a mushroom cellar."

Mackenzie reached for her Pepsi. A big bug raced out from beneath a stack of papers next to it. "Roach!" Mackenzie yelled, accidentally knocking over the can of soda.

The six-inch-long African cockroach jumped onto the floor and darted for cover. Mackenzie snapped back from the scare, took off her left shoe, and clobbered the bug as it headed for a radiator. "A bunch of them escaped from Dr. Farr's collections last year and she had been hunting them down ever since," Mackenzie explained.

The blood had drained from my face.

"P.C. doesn't like roaches," Mackenzie told Spiegelman as she looked for something to wipe up the bug and spilled soda. "It's just his thing."

Spiegelman shifted his wheelchair into position so he could open the middle metal closet. He grabbed a handful of paper towels that sat on top of the reams of copy paper and spare printer cartridges, and helped Mackenzie blot up the spill.

"I hope I didn't ruin anything important," Mackenzie said.

"I don't think there could be any crucial evidence the police missed, do you?" Spiegelman said.

The color had returned to my face and I spoke up. "Dr. Spiegelman, the newsletter said your specialty was Indian antiquities. That you were headhunted from the Vancouver Museum because of the Ganesh necklace."

"You have a good memory, P.C.," Spiegelman said. "Specifically, I was hired to come here to oversee the premiere display of the necklace. It's the first time the royal family of Rajasthan has allowed it out of the country. I was the only one the family would release the necklace to."

"It must be a very cool necklace," Mackenzie said.

"It is exquisite and without peer," Spiegelman said. "It's the 'gala gimmick,' Dr. Gardner calls it."

Spiegelman checked the camcorder in my hand once more and did a repeat of his big smile. "Well," he said, "good luck with your remarkable theory."

"Dr. Spiegelman," I said, "would you mind telling us where you were at the time Dr. Farr was strangled?"

Spiegelman laughed. "You're kidding," he said.

"No, we're not," I said.

"Well—let me see," Spiegelman said rolling his eyes upward like most people do when they think, for some reason. "I believe I was in my office preparing a display tray of our Australian opals. You know, arranging them in order of their color and inner fire."

"Was anyone helping you?" I asked.

"No," he said. "In fact, I had the door to my office locked. Even if someone knocks I don't answer when I have any of the gem trays out of the vault. That would be asking for trouble, I'm afraid."

"Of course," I said. The three of us exchanged glances and I could tell we were all thinking there was no air-tight alibi here.

Spiegelman shifted his wheelchair and whirred quickly out of the office. After a minute I heard the clanging of the elevator door and its inner gate opening and closing, and the room was silent again except for the rustling of the insects crawling over twigs and shredded paper. I took out my cell phone and pressed the memory button to dial Jesus's number. The signal went through. Jesus answered.

"Add Liam Spiegelman's name to the top of the suspect list," I said. "Right up there with Mirsky and Congers. I'll explain later."

"Hey, why'd you say that?" Mackenzie asked after I'd disconnected. "Spiegelman's a nice guy."

"Yes, but he's got one little flaw."

"What?"

"He knows Farr's office pretty well—better than he'd have us believe."

"How could you know that?"

"Basics," I said. "He knew where she kept her paper towels. He went straight for them in the middle cabinet."

"So he's a liar?"

"You got it," I said. A little voice inside me told me

something else. "Oh," I went on, "and give Spalding Kazinski a call on your phone now. Tell him that we've become really fascinated by the Ganesh legends. Yes, tell him we want to know *all* about the Indian god."

## Greed

**With the case going to the District Attorney** in the morning, Mackenzie and I shifted into high gear. She called her mom and had her line up clearance for us to see Tom at five o'clock. Sundays the jail has regular visiting hours anyway, but Mrs. Riggs pulled strings to make certain there wouldn't be any unannounced visits by Mrs. Boggs. From there, I had wanted to get back up to the West Side, muster with Jesus, and catch Mirsky's lecture at the Ethical Culture auditorium at eight.

"I want to hear him, too," Mackenzie said. "I just know he'll probably make Freudian slips all over the place."

"Positive," I said. "There's nothing more dangerous for anyone with something to hide than giving a lecture."

We left Farr's office and headed out to the lobby. "Why do you think Spiegelman lied about knowing Farr and his way around her office?" I asked.

"Maybe he didn't want to be involved in a murder case," Mackenzie said. "Lots of people clam up when someone gets knocked off, even if they're not guilty of anything. And from what you said, one meeting with Krakowski would be enough to gag a ghoul."

"It's probably more likely Spiegelman was blowing hot air up Farr's smock to get a grant. That's what everyone else around this place seems to have been doing."

"Hey, he might have been dating her."

"You've got to be kidding," I said, but I knew that in Manhattan when it comes to freaky romances anything was possible.

We left via the museum's rear entrance to Columbus Avenue, and I led the way straight to the Cosmic Café Annex.

"I need a protein fix before jail," I said.

"Me, too," Mackenzie said.

When we got to the Cosmic, we sat at the counter because it would be the quickest way to get served. Mackenzie likes her hamburgers well-done so she can forget she's eating ground-up pieces of cow. Sometimes she does turkey or veggie burgers or a Jupiter FishamaJig or whatever they call them. I like my burgers rare with globs of melting Roquefort cheese oozing all over them. Mackenzie also ordered the Constellation fries and I got an order of Cajun Moon onion rings. When the food came, we wolfed everything down, scooted to the corner of 86th and CPW, and grabbed the train back downtown again.

When we came up from the subway, the Avenue of the Finest and Police Plaza was fairly empty. Inside the jail, a different reception guard and matron frisked us, X-rayed our backpacks, and checked out the camcorder. Finally, they issued us our passes.

As we went down the hallway, practically all the police workers looked like they were having a party or waiting desperately for their next coffee break. A lot were joking with each other like a lot of City workers do, and a few of them were gabbing loudly on phones. They were saying things like, "Hey, *Nosferatu* doesn't start until eight-ten," and "You know, it wouldn't kill you if you picked up some Colonel's Extra Crispy on the way home tonight."

One room we passed looked like a half-dozen plain-clothes detectives. Two of them had their feet up on their desks and were watching a hockey game on TV. One of the other detectives was checking the horse-racing charts in the afternoon *Post*. "Hey, that was close," one in an orange blazer shouted to another. "I was only one off on the Daily Pick Four." Whatever, the whole scene made us feel all the more sorry for Tom. If he didn't have us in his corner, it was pretty clear that there'd be no one to police the police.

The same cop who looked like he was on heavy-duty steroids led us to the visiting room. He was reading a self-help paperback called *Why Am I Dancing Alone? Here's How to Find and Keep Someone to Love.*

Mackenzie and I took our usual seats at the big heavy table. They kept us waiting nearly twenty minutes before we saw Tom being led down the hall. He was escorted by the Hispanic guard with the ponytail. The good news is that this time Tom wasn't handcuffed. He looked a little weak but not depressed like he had looked on our first visit. "Your mother must have gotten through to somebody," I whispered to Mackenzie.

"I told her the way Tom looked," Mackenzie said. "She said she'd pull every string she could so that they'd treat him okay."

The guard opened the gate and brought Tom into the room. Like the guard did the last time, he sat Tom in the chair at the end of the table. "You've got ten minutes," the guard told us, and retreated to his corner.

Mackenzie and I wiggled our chairs closer. "How's it going, Tom?" Mackenzie asked, as I was busy setting up the camcorder.

"Okay," Tom said. "Thanks for coming, guys." His eyes were a little red but the tremor in his hands and jaw had disappeared. He smiled faintly as he fidgeted with the cross that hung around his neck. "My lawyer says I should accept a plea bargain," Tom said, his voice barely audible.

"You can't do that," I said. "You're innocent."

"We don't know that," Tom said. "The lawyer says if I accept a lesser murder charge—he said something about manslaughter—I don't know—he said it'd be best.

He said too many people saw me choking Dr. Farr."

Mackenzie looked to me, then said, "Don't do it, Tom. You didn't kill anyone. We know that. We just *know* it. . . ."

"We don't have much time, Tom," I said. "We're trying to do everything we can to find out what really happened at the museum. We made a video that we want you to look at. Maybe it will jog your memory."

"A video of what?"

"You'll see."

While I fiddled with rewinding the tape in the camera, Mackenzie quizzed Tom with other stuff we needed to know. "We were told you helped Spiegelman set up stuff in the Hall of Minerals. Did you also do anything for Dr. Mirsky or Beverly Congers? Did either of them ever ask you to help in their offices or anywhere?"

"Sure," Tom said. "I do a lot of things for a lot of people."

"Exactly what did you do lately for Mirsky or Congers?" Mackenzie pressed.

Tom thought a moment. "I emptied their wastepaper baskets. I mopped Mirsky's floors. Jimmy Tater mops Congers's office, but she always asks me to open her windows—and she's been having trouble with her thermostat." Tom thought a moment longer and looked pleased he thought of something else. "And Dr. Mirsky asked me to wash his Toyota."

"His *car*?" I said. "You're not supposed to wash any-one's car."

"He said I should."

Mackenzie was really ticked off. "You know, Di Pietro, the shop teacher at Westside School, got caught forcing a class to make a credenza for his girlfriend's apartment, and he got fired."

"I changed her worm beds, too," Tom said. "Congers's."

"*What* worm beds?" Mackenzie asked.

"The ones in her office that clean fresh skull and bone specimens. You know, those kind."

"Cleaning worm beds should be her job, not yours," I said.

"Yeah, but she doesn't like maggots," Tom said. "She brought me a big box of chocolate-covered Dutch pretzels for helping her. Worm beds don't smell as awful as you might think, you know."

"Nice," Mackenzie said.

"All right, Tom," I said. "Just watch *this*." I pressed the replay button and the image of Mackenzie sweeping the lobby flickered onto the camera's screen. Tom stared at the playback.

"You're a good sweeper," Tom told Mackenzie, and laughed. Mackenzie and I laughed with him, just like we used to do when the three of us would share tuna fish roll-ups in the park or stop for nonfat angel food cake and coffee.

"Tell us anything you remember." I said. "Anything that pops into your head about that Friday . . ."

Tom watched Mackenzie's image maneuvering the broom. I had forgotten how the camera's mike would pick up the sound of me shooting commands to Mackenzie. I always hate the sound of my voice. I was grateful when the background sounds of the nuns in the tour group and the music from the Death of the Universe began to creep in and drown out my droning.

The smile slowly disappeared from Tom's face.

"What's the matter?" Mackenzie asked.

Tom didn't answer. He began to fidget and rub his hands. A coldness moved into his eyes and he started to squirm in his chair.

"What do you see?" I asked him.

The background music from the planetarium show swelled, and with it Tom slowly stood up like a trembling zombie. I signaled the guards to stay back, and put my hand on Tom's shoulder. He settled back into his seat.

"It's the music," I said. "We lucked into the hypnotic trigger!"

"Tom, that's what it is, isn't it?" Mackenzie asked. "The *music*?"

I don't think Tom could even hear us. He looked anxious. Frustrated—like he needed to go someplace. He began to make whining sounds like a frightened puppy. His whimpering quieted as he watched Mackenzie in the video lay down the broom and turn to start walking down Hallway C. Tom looked spaced out, watching her pause in front of Conchetta's doorway.

The whining began again.

"He's been programmed, all right," I told Mackenzie. She nodded.

"It could be at least a two-part trigger, maybe three parts," I said. "The music might be the first part, to get him to go to Farr's lab. But there's got to be something else. Another trigger."

"What?" Mackenzie asked.

"Whoever programmed him had to pick something that would happen as predictably as the music at the end of the Death of the Universe show. Some second trigger that the killer could count on when Tom went to Conchetta's office."

"When Tom *saw* Conchetta," Mackenzie said.

"Right."

"A word," Mackenzie said. "The killer could have known a word that would always be said. Or a phrase. Something he could depend upon Conchetta or Tom saying. Or if the killer were there, he could have delivered the trigger himself. He could have been hiding. He could have been somewhere in the lab. It had to be something really weird like that."

"I think so."

Mackenzie is always better than I am at anything to do with words. I'm good at riddles, but she's the expert with anything to do with vocabulary. She always knocks the stuffing out of me when we play Scrabble.

"*Hello, Conchetta*," Mackenzie said to Tom, testing the words. There was no reaction.

"That's not it," I said. "Just free-associate." I started blurting out words into Tom's face. "*Hallway. Doctor. Farr . . .*"

Nothing.

"*How are you, Dr. Farr? Hello, Bug Lady.*" Mackenzie began to raise her voice, saying every word and phrase that came to her. She took a deep breath. *Cockroaches. Scorpions. Centipedes.* The guards were on high alert now, inching closer to us. I knew at any second they'd blow the whistle and make us leave.

"*Food. Larvae. Worms . . .*" I was beginning to bray at Tom, too. Tom was squirming, but his eyes now looked frozen in terror, as if there were a terrible battle of wills going on inside of him.

"*Nice day. Office. Pretty dress . . .*" Mackenzie was still rapid-firing.

"*Aristotle, big spider, hairy spider . . .*" I said.

*Tarantula* was no sooner out of my mouth than Mackenzie and I looked at each other. The identical thought had struck us both at the same time, but she shouted it first.

"Spider Woman!" Mackenzie shot at Tom. "Spider Woman!"

There was a frightening growling, then a series of

rapidly mounting shrieks like you'd hear in a monkey house. The sounds came from Tom, and he spun to face Mackenzie. Before I could stop him, his hands shot out at her like clowns from jack-in-the-boxes.

Mackenzie screamed as Tom's hands locked around her throat. I threw myself onto Tom's back, chopping at his arms to break his hold—but for the moment he had the strength of a bear. The guards were on Tom now, trying to pry his fingers loose from around Mackenzie's neck.

They began to club him.

"No!" Mackenzie cried out. "He's not choking me," she was screaming now. "Don't hurt him! He's not *choking* me!"

A few moments more and the guards had broken Tom's grip. I was aware of someone in blue and a rainbow-colored jacket charging into the room from behind a mirrored door. The voice was strident. Loud. Familiar. "Take him away," the squat woman ordered. "Get him out of here."

The guards dragged Tom off as Lieutenant Krakowski strode toward us, snapping her head so that her china-doll hair flew askew and then fell back into perfect shape. "You two snoops are over your heads," she said furiously. "Way over your heads. You don't know what you've gotten yourselves into. That little pal of yours is psychotic, and you don't mess with that. Do either of you know what that means? Psychotic! Do you?"

"But he wasn't actually choking me," Mackenzie repeated clearly. *"He really wasn't."*

## 11

### A Stalk in the Park

**"His hands were around my throat,** but he wasn't hurting me," Mackenzie kept insisting.

Lieutenant Krakowski snorted and roared at Mackenzie. "He was strangling you the same way he strangled Dr. Farr, that's what he was doing!"

"*Exactly* the same way," I said, wedging myself between Krakowski and Mackenzie. "He was able to be hypnotized—programmed!—to put his hands around Conchetta Farr when anyone said 'Spider Woman!' But that was all his conscience would let him do. Tom didn't have it in him to really choke anyone—so the real murderer framed him as best he could. The killer set it up so witnesses would see Tom with his hands around Conchetta's throat and they'd think he had choked her to death."

Krakowski's eyes glazed over with fury and frustration as I shot words at her like bullets from an Uzi. I explained the triggers, and how the real killer must have known the precise time when he'd have to do the actual choking—five, maybe ten minutes before the end of the planetarium show. If she had made any sounds, he probably smothered them. Then, when the killer saw Tom coming to the lab, he used the second trigger, Spider Woman! Tom was programmed to think he was putting a necklace around Farr's throat or measuring her for a scarf. It had to be something innocent—at least an action that the killer made him *believe* was harmless. Anything that would get the hypnotized Tom to put his hands around Conchetta's neck and scream. It was probably Tom's *scream* everyone heard. All the killer had to do was position Conchetta's body in the chair. Tom wouldn't have known she was already a corpse.

"You know, kid," Krakowski said. "You're giving me a headache."

"Egads, forensics must have told you about the adrenoreceptor found in Tom's blood," I said. "Don't you see how Tom was set up!"

"What I saw just now is a young man attack a teenage girl, that's what I saw," Lieutenant Krakowski snapped back. She made a gesture to the guards and in a moment they flanked Mackenzie and me and started marching us out of the room.

"He wasn't hurting me," Mackenzie yelled over her shoulder.

I pressed eject on the camcorder. It spit out the videotape and I tossed it to Krakowski. She caught it like it was a hot brick. "Check out the triggers on Tom! Check them!"

"You troublemakers keep out of this case," Lieutenant Krakowski roared, red-faced. "And stay away from that museum and anything to do with this case or I'll arrest the pair of you for obstruction of justice. Don't think for a second that I won't!"

The door closed on her yelping, and Mackenzie and I were escorted straight out to the street. We didn't say anything more until we had crossed the deserted Avenue of the Finest and were heading back down into the subway.

"God, she's a judicial witch," Mackenzie said, slapping on her shades and straightening the fringe on her fake-leopard shoulder bag. "Talk about out of control."

"I'd love to squeeze the juice out of *two* halves of a grapefruit on her *ears*," I said.

"I guess now we know what we're dealing with," Mackenzie said. "Tom was definitely hypnotized by a henna-tinged drug. Farr was more than likely already dead and propped up in her chair by the time Tom got to her lab. And I agree with you now that the Ganesh necklace probably is somehow involved."

"That's what I think," I said. "And as far as our suspects and motives, Mirsky's got Farr's job. Congers is mad as a hornet and probably hated Farr as much as anyone. And Dr. Spiegelman is a liar."

"What a crew," Mackenzie said. "Whoever is behind all of this has got to be one vicious, greedy lunatic, so we're going to do what Lieutenant Krakowski wants:

stay away from the museum. Right?"

"Not a chance."

"I didn't think so."

It was around six-thirty by the time we got up to the Lopezes' brownstone on the corner of West 73rd and Riverside Drive. Jesus was out in front in his low-tech wheelchair going through one of his notebooks that was spread wide on his lap. He gave a big wave when he saw us coming down the street.

"You're late," he said, tossing his long black hair out of his eyes and propelling his chair with his strong arms to meet us. "I was afraid they were going to keep you down at the jail." Jesus is thirteen, but he's been a computer whiz for years.

"We were afraid they'd lock us up and throw away the key," Mackenzie admitted.

I took over pushing Jesus's wheelchair while Mackenzie filled him in on the weird and freaky developments in the case up to the moment, including Tom's reaction to the video and our locking horns with Krakowski—and the possibility that the whole case had something to do with the gala and the museum's jewels.

"The murderer could be after a lot of the other pieces in the permanent collection," Jesus said. "The Star of India sapphire or the Egyptian rubies."

"They have jewelry that even belonged to Napoleon and Josephine," Mackenzie said.

"A lot more stuff than the Ganesh necklace," I agreed. "But the necklace is the newest piece, so it must figure in here somewhere. Also, apparently it's one of the most valuable pieces of jewelry in the world."

Today we still had a good hour before Mackenzie and I had to be at Ethical Culture, so we decided to take our usual circle route starting from Strawberry Fields on West 72nd, then south around the Central Park Carousel, and north again to the Alice-in-Wonderland statue at the sailboat pond (which is officially called the *Conservatory Water* pond, but most people don't know or care about that). Jesus started going over everything he'd dug up on Mirsky, Congers, and Spiegelman as we could hear the carousel's calliope playing "Crying on the Outside" and, aptly, "Tie a Yellow Ribbon 'Round the Old Oak Tree."

Jesus pulled out a brown, worn accordion file from one of the wheelchair's saddlebags. He had outfitted the whole chair like an office on wheels. "Like you asked, I kept an eye out for anything on the main suspects that had anything to do with mind control. Hypnosis. Any stuff like that. There was the most wacky stuff on Mirsky."

"Like what?" I asked.

Jesus took out a beret, set it on his head, and pushed his hair up into it. "Mirsky never seems to have been satisfied with straight paleontology," he said. "The impression you get from the journals and interviews I've been able to pull up on the Web is that one month he'd stick to what he knew—discoveries from the middle Paleozoic era—and then he'd go off on a tangent and publish something loony like an article on the existence of UFOs in the backgrounds of Renaissance paintings. He's a big joiner, you know, is on a lot of boards like the Metropolitan Opera and Roundabout Theater. Stuff like that. And he's taken an awful lot of trips to Haiti."

"Haiti has voodoo," Mackenzie said.

"Exactly my thinking," Jesus said. "I checked out that lead. Mirsky collects Haitian art. He's studied Haitian culture, including voodoo. The journals show he's taken courses in it. Written about it. He's got, like, voodoo on the brain. He did a master's thesis on the magical and curative abilities of voodoo doctors. Some really twisted stuff."

"I checked his records at the museum, and he's been to North Africa within the last six months," I said. "He could have bought any kind of drugs."

Mackenzie took over pushing Jesus's wheelchair up the Promenade of the Discoverers, a cobblestone walkway lined with benches and statues of famous dead people like Shakespeare and Madame Curie. "What about Congers?" she asked. "What did you find out about her?"

"Oh, she's a weirdo in her own right," Jesus said. "I checked the dates of her published articles, and it really does look like she did double time to keep up with

Mirsky. Every time he published one of his flying saucer or voodoo articles, Congers would come out with something just as bananas under the banner of cultural anthropology."

"*How* eccentric?" I wanted to know.

Jesus pulled out another file from the wheelchair's left saddlebag. "Let's see," he said, thumbing through his printouts. "Once she researched skeletons and mummies in the catacombs of St. Cecelia's Cathedral in Galati. She ended up publishing sworn statements by a hundred members of the congregation that said they had seen a vision of Joan of Arc appear on the altar, shouting 'Women will rule the earth!' Everything Congers writes has sort of an afterlife feminist spin on it."

"She's been to North Africa three times this year," I said.

A shock of Jesus's hair slipped out from beneath his beret and fell down into his eyes. He pushed it back up and under. "American anthropology shows she's done a lot of respected scientific work, but her weakness is mysticism," he said. "A few years ago she wrote *Journey to the Light*, a pop anthropology book about reincarnation that sold like hotcakes and got her into *Who's Who of American Women*."

"What about Spiegelman?" I asked when we arrived at the sailboat pond.

The benches around the rim of the pond were

Mackenzie's and my favorite place to hang out in all of Central Park. We always went there to have long talks about death, school, friendship, parents, love, movies, books, and CDs. We talked about anything we could think of, actually.

There were hordes of old men sailing all kinds of miniature remote-controlled boats. A few kids were putting pieces of corn dogs on strings and luring crawfish up from the murky bottom of the pond. Dozens of toddlers and their mothers climbed and played on the shiny brass mushrooms and granite rocks of the Alice-in-Wonderland and Hans Christian Andersen statues.

We settled in around a table next to an ice-cream stand.

"There's not much on Spiegelman, just that he's an Indian antiquities expert and a reclusive author," Jesus said. "He just seems to really love India and its art and culture."

"He has a top-of-the-line motorized wheelchair," Mackenzie said. "I wish we were rich so we could get you one."

Jesus laughed. "I do, too."

He scanned his notes for any other details. "Mirsky's got a wife and a Great Dane. No kids. They live in Westchester. Congers lives in Brooklyn Heights with two parrots and has been divorced for years. And Spiegelman's single."

"No really weird stuff?"

"Not really."

We watched the men with the racing boats manipulating the switches on their remote-control boxes. The boats sailed and listed and rolled around a set of tiny buoys at the far end of the pond, then started the journey back. An Oriental man launched a six-foot exact replica of the *Santa Maria*. I noticed Mackenzie staring at the galleon, with its elaborate sails and riggings. Jesus and I jumped when she suddenly let her right leg shoot up into the air, kicking off her shoe.

"Oh, my God," Mackenzie cried.

"What?" Jesus and I wanted to know.

We looked at her foot expecting to see a big bug or something. Instead, she was pointing at a small red butterfly she had tattooed on her ankle. "My tattoo," she said.

"What about it?" I said.

"It's a henna tattoo," she said. "You know—*mehendi* tattoos—all that Indian decorative art! The henna-tinged drug could have come from India, too. We've got to recheck the museum staff for any connections to India."

"And to the Ganesh necklace," I said.

"Exactly," Mackenzie said. "Just like that."

"This whole case is like one big logic puzzle," I said pushing Jesus's wheelchair on our way back along the 72nd Street transverse.

"I hate those puzzles," Mackenzie said.

As we passed the Bethesda Fountain and headed up

the slope, I slowed and stiffened. Mackenzie picked up on the change right away. "What's the matter?" she asked.

I knew it would look weird, but I did a little skip, laughed loudly, and started singing, apparently for no good reason.

Mackenzie and Jesus stared at me like I was nuts, but caught on and joined right in. We always switch into a fake animated mode when we think someone's spying on us.

"*He's there*," I whispered through a wide, put-on grin. "He's watching us."

"Who?" Jesus asked.

"The druggie kid Gardner pointed out to me from his office window."

"Where?" Mackenzie asked, pretending to need to adjust her sunglasses and scratch her nose.

"Next to the Falconer statue."

Mackenzie raised her glance slowly. I watched as her eyes met the stare of the kid on the ridge. He was wearing the same gray-and-blue camouflage pants pulled down low on his waist. His hair was greased and spiked into an even larger chrysanthemum. He stared down at *us*.

Mackenzie exhaled. "He looks like one nasty piece of work," she said.

"Ditto," Jesus said.

A moment later when I glanced back up to the ridge, the druggie was gone.

## 12

### Attack

**Jesus took off** to check on the connections to India of everyone on the museum staff. Time was growing short, so Mackenzie and I headed straight down Central Park West to the Ethical Culture auditorium at 65th Street.

The whole Ethical Culture Society is always doing things to shake people up, like founding the NAACP or the American Civil Liberties Union. My mom and dad used to tell me about hearing famous people like Bruno Bettelheim and Saul Bellow speak in the auditorium there. What impressed me was the fact that J. Robert Oppenheimer, the physicist who led the research team that built the first atomic bomb, went to the elementary school there.

Any of the lectures I had gone to at Ethical always had a big turnout. But not tonight. It was five minutes to eight o'clock when Mackenzie and I ran up the front steps and into the lobby. There was a big picture of Dr. Jeffrey Mirsky on a tripod in front of the main entrance, with the title of his talk in big red letters plastered across the top: "Fossils of Death: Comforts in the Tomb."

"What a revolting topic," Mackenzie said.

"It sure is," I said. "Let's sit in the front row."

I led the way down an aisle on the left of the auditorium.

"If he's the killer, it's as if he's flaunting the murder in our faces," Mackenzie said. "It's like Jack the Ripper sending notes to the detectives in Scotland Yard saying *Please Catch Me*."

I grunted as we grabbed seats. The auditorium was old, with curving rows, elaborate moldings, and balconies like Albert Hall in London.

The lights dimmed at 8 P.M. sharp. There were only a few dozen people in the auditorium, mostly ladies with blue hair, and men with wigs and hearing aids. Mirsky came strutting out with a toothy smile and looking spiffy in a black pinstriped suit. He went to the podium, set his handful of three-by-five cards down next to a glass of water and adjusted the microphone.

He checked the balcony. I turned to see what he was staring at, and elbowed Mackenzie. "There's Congers," I said.

"What's *she* doing up there?" Mackenzie said.

"People appear to have been interested in fossils since the earliest of times," Mirsky began. "It is remarkable how many fossils have been found buried with the remains of prehistoric humans. During the Dark Ages, fossils were explained alternately as the remains of special creation, freaks of nature, and devices that Satan placed in rocks to lead people astray . . ."

Mackenzie leaned forward, planting her elbows on her knees. She was listening carefully to Mirsky's every word.

"It wasn't until the Renaissance that the true nature of fossils was accepted by scholars and the educated of the world," Mirsky yakked on. "Ironically, it was Leonardo da Vinci who became very much interested in the fossils found in tombs of Cro-Magnon ice mummies. . . ."

Mirsky continued, his voice alternately arched and hesitant. After ten minutes or so, watching his artificial smile and listening to his creepy content began to make me sleepy. For a while he made strange sounds trying to clear his voice, and it drove me loony for a half hour watching him do that before he finally reached out to the glass of water on the podium, lifted it to his lips, and took a sip.

The moment he lifted the glass, Mackenzie and I noticed a sudden movement along the edge of the podium heading for where Mirsky's left hand was planted. It seemed at first like a shadow—black—moving. Mirsky seemed unaware of the motion.

I think for a moment Mackenzie and I thought we were seeing things, but when the thin form snaked its way onto Mirsky's hand and began to wiggle and swirl its way up the sleeve of his suit, we knew what it was. It was easy to recognize as one of the larger poisonous centipedes we'd always seen in Conchetta's lab.

Mirsky could feel the centipede now, something racing up toward his shoulders. He patted his arm gently at first, as if he was having a muscle spasm, but soon he realized it was a living thing.

"Centipede!" Mackenzie cried out.

For a moment, everyone in the audience looked at her like she was insane.

I was on my feet now, and we were both heading to the stage as the centipede burst up from under Mirsky's white collar and began to circle his throat. Mirsky let out a high-pitched scream, slapping at the thing climbing up the side of his face. One of the slaps connected and the long, writhing bug was propelled toward the audience. Everyone saw the centipede land in front of the stage and begin to race into the seats. People were screaming everywhere, but Mackenzie, a patent-leather platform shoe held high, was closing in fast on the bug. It was crawling up the back of a chair in the second row when she connected, her heel squashing the bug's head.

For a while its body still twitched, but Mackenzie scooped it onto one of Mirsky's programs and dumped them both in a trash bin.

"The police," Mirsky was shouting. "I want the police. Someone tried to kill me. . . ."

I checked the balcony, but Congers was gone. It took a good fifteen minutes before the police arrived, two chunky-looking guys who looked like they'd had their nightly snoozing interrupted. Mirsky made them find the centipede's body. He kept telling them that somehow somebody had planted it in a small box under the lip of the podium with the water glass pressed against one end of it. When he lifted the water glass, the bug was able to scoot out of the box and attack him.

"Someone wants me dead, and I want you to *do* something about it!" Mirsky shouted.

One of the cops was holding back giggles while he was writing up the report, until Mirsky screamed right into his face, "I'm from the museum! I work where we had the murder. The murder, you idiots! The murder!"

Then the cops took things a bit more seriously. A few other underling cops arrived and began to make sure everyone else left the auditorium. "Just go home everyone. Sorry. Lecture's over. . . ."

Mackenzie was trembling slightly as I took her arm and we went down the steep steps back out onto 64th Street. She does that a lot, you know—springs into action like Jamie Lee Curtis protecting herself against her crazy brother in *Halloween*—and then trembles later when she gets a chance to think about what really happened.

"Somebody planted that bug," Mackenzie said. "It's like the ghost of Conchetta was arranging a type of poetic justice—although I guess this knocks Mirsky out as a suspect. Whoever planted the centipede has to be the same one who killed Conchetta."

"We don't know that," I said. "We do still need to check an alibi on him. Where was he when Conchetta got it? Anytime there's a murder there's a lot of copycat stuff that pops up all around the place. Someone could just be taking advantage of one killer's murder to chalk up one of his or her own. However, whoever arranged for that centipede surprise knew exactly what kind of bug to take from Conchetta's collection. They knew which was the most dangerous."

A cool, stiff breeze was blowing down Central Park West as we headed up toward Mackenzie's place.

"Hey, she used to broadcast that certain bugs from her collection could kill you with one bite," Mackenzie said. "She was proud of it. It's got to be Congers, who hates Mirsky's guts anyway. She had that weird look on her face tonight. Well, Congers *or* Spiegelman, one of the two."

"Not necessarily."

"What are you talking about?"

"It could have been Mirsky who planted the centipede."

"Trying to kill *himself*?"

"No," I said. "He would have known even if he'd gotten bitten he'd have been rushed to Roosevelt Hospital, less than ten blocks away. He'd know they have antidotes there for every bite from a New York State rattlesnake to a rabid Tasmanian devil. There's always somebody in a supermarket getting bitten from something hiding in a bunch of imported artichokes or bananas."

"So what are you saying?"

"Mirsky could have wanted to divert attention from himself as a suspect. Cops arrive at murders every day where the killer's inflicted a knife or gun wound on himself and yelling, 'Somebody tried to knock me off. Somebody tried to knock me off.'"

"Okay, I buy that," Mackenzie said. "But how does this connect to your greed theory?"

"I don't know yet. Maybe it doesn't," I said. "Maybe it doesn't at all. All I know is that we've got to prove Tom's innocent and get him out of jail."

Mackenzie started to cry softly. We both wanted Tom to be able to go home and sleep in his own bed. She stopped and pulled a tissue out of her bag and dabbed at her eyes. "I don't know which is worse, if Congers set that centipede to get Mirsky, or if our killer just hasn't stopped killing yet."

## 13

### Sticks and Stones

**I didn't catch up with Mackenzie** until Monday during third period at the Westside School. She had physics and an acting class in the morning while I was in advanced chem, followed by a chef's class I took as an elective because it'd be stress free, and it wouldn't hurt if I knew how to make a meat loaf. Third period we met in the school newspaper office. We were freelance reviewers for *The Crow's Nest*, mainly because Miss Conlan is the faculty adviser and she lets us keep a lot of the free books and theater tickets that loads of publishers and producers send. Also, third period was great, because nobody else used the office then, so we could just hang out like it was our private VIP lounge.

"Spalding cornered me in acting class," Mackenzie said, coming into the office clutching two sets of stapled papers. "He's downloaded everything he could find on Ganesh. Pictures of him with his elephant head and how he travels around on a mouse. All kinds of stuff." She tossed one of the sets to me.

"Thanks," I said catching the set. "Did you read it?"

"Yeah, I had a lot of time," Mackenzie said. "Mr. Raposo didn't show up—something weird about him going to Las Vegas over the weekend and his plane getting engine trouble—but we think he probably made that up. Wendy Fillerman said he's picked *Cabaret* as the spring musical and that she's been promised the lead. Spalding asked her if she'd forgotten to take her medication today."

I was sitting in front of one of the office computers with a full-screen color shot of Ganesh. I was glad Spalding had downloaded a mess of stuff, because I felt there was something very important about the Ganesh necklace that we didn't know yet. I had had the feeling all morning that it was as if Mackenzie and I were climbing a mountain—that we were at the base camp and about to make the final assault on the peak. The picture in front of me was of Ganesh holding a conch shell, a discus, a club, and a lotus flower. "How'd he get the elephant's head?" I asked.

"Oh, that part is so horrible it makes me want to engage in reverse peristalsis," Mackenzie said. She sat in one of the desk chairs and rolled it next to me. "First of all, everybody in India loves Ganesh. He's the god of wisdom and prudence and salvation, and practically everything."

"Sounds like the kind of god Tom needs."

"That's what I thought. Anyway, Ganesh is India's favorite god. He's on all the country's happy occasion

cards, and his image is at weddings and birth announce-
ments. I mean, they adore him and invoke his name all
the time. He's right up there with our 'Gesundheit' and
'God bless you.'"

"But what about his weird head?"

"Oh, yes. Well, the story *there* is that once upon a time
he was a normal, really good-looking young boy," she
said, flipping through her set of papers. "And he was
guarding his mother's door while she was taking a
bath—see, she asked him to—and when his father tried
to get past, Ganesh wouldn't let him, so his father took
an ax and chopped the boy's head off. Just whacked it so
it rolled across the floor."

"That's really vicious. . . ."

"Yes, that's what his mother, Parvati, thought, too, so
she got very depressed and nagged and bugged her
husband, Shiva, so much, that Shiva ordered his guards
to cut off the head of the first living being that was
found. . . ."

"And it turned out to be an elephant?"

"Right—a baby elephant—or as they call them, a *calf*,"
Mackenzie said. "Shiva placed the elephant head on
Ganesh's body and restored him to life."

"That poor kid," I said. Then I started to flip through
Spalding's papers.

"There's the whole story of Ganesh traveling around
the world in there, too," Mackenzie said. "It's like the
most famous story about Ganesh." She reached over

and opened my set to a particular page. "*Here*," she said, pointing out a paragraph.

> *A legend explains why Ganesh is worshiped more than all other Indian deities. It is because he is clever and a trickster. One day Shiva told Ganesh and his brother, Kartikeya, to go around the world—and whoever circled the globe the fastest would inherit all of his kingdom. Kartikeya took off to spend the six weeks it would take to go around the world on his magical peacock—but Ganesh simply walked around his parents. He explained to his father and mother that they were the world to him—and so they gave him all their money and the whole kingdom.*

"See," Mackenzie said, "Ganesh always does neat stuff like that. He plays jokes. He's so smart. That's why so many people love him in India. He's like a supercool guy even with his elephant head."

There was a rapping on the door. We saw Spalding's wide-eyed, intense face staring at us like he was trapped in a washing machine. His hair was cut into straight bangs in a style you see in movies about mental patients.

"Whaddya want?" I called out.

Mackenzie pinched me, got up, and opened the door. "We were just going over your stuff," she told Spalding. "It's really a terrific beginning for our project."

"Yes," I said. "Nice work."

Spalding smiled, which I thought always made him

really look like Milo the Donkey Boy. "I just wanted you to know I put a lot of time into it already, and I was thinking there's something you guys could do that would help us get an A."

"Surprise us," I said.

Spalding looked like he wanted to stab me with a pencil. "You could get us into the museum to see the necklace. We'd be able to preview it and get brochures—or take a tape recorder, just put all our impressions down like we were Eyewitness News or somebody. Maybe even do a multimedia presentation. Power Point. Something flashy. That's the kind of thing that gets Miss Conlan really excited," Spalding said. "You know, something visual."

"Not going to happen," I said. "They're not letting anyone see the necklace until tomorrow night."

"Well, then, hey," Spalding said, "you could at least get some of the museum's press photos of it. They've got to be handing out press kits with all that stuff in it. That museum does that for even the opening of an envelope."

"Nope," I said. "The Ganesh necklace won't be photographed until the gala. There will be plenty of photographs then."

Spalding pouted. "You're not even trying. I mean, I've done all our research, and if you could get some inside spin on everything, it's worth extra credit. That's going to look good on our college applications, and you know it. You may want to get stuck going to some place like Baton Rouge or Albany, but I'm not."

It took us until just before the bell rang to get rid of Kazinski. When he left, I was muttering, "He really bugs me, he really does . . ." and putting the Ganesh research into my backpack. Mackenzie repeated Aunt Doris's favorite little piece of wisdom about how *it's an ill wind that doesn't blow someone some good*—when I noticed the copy of the newspaper article that we'd found in Conchetta Farr's copy machine. I'd forgotten I'd stuck it in a large zipper compartment between a notebook and my world history textbook. I took it out and unfolded it carefully on the sunlit desk.

"Egads." The faded, old article about the Galveston school bus accident now held me riveted.

"What?" Mackenzie asked. She checked the date. "That accident was over thirty years ago."

It took her a moment longer before she saw in the article's photo what I should have seen from the beginning. The caption still held no familiar names, but the photo of the bus driver was of a young man we did know. At least we knew him now, three decades after the photo had been taken.

"It's Gardner," I said.

Mackenzie peered closer. "It certainly is."

We read the article carefully now. Gardner was twenty-four in the photo, and according to the caption, his name had been Chad Taylor Young. He was driving a school bus and it flipped over on a dirt road. He crashed the bus and seven children were injured, a couple of them very seriously. One little girl had lost her legs.

"He was drunk," Mackenzie said, reading the details. "It says he was drunk and driving too fast on a curve."

"And Conchetta knew about it," I said.

"She not only knew about it, she dug up this article on Gardner and *saved* it."

"At least we know now how she got appointed head of research," I said. "We're going to have to pay Dr. Gardner another little visit," I added, as we stepped out into the horde of kids zigzagging through the halls. "Pronto."

109

14

## A Worm Is the Only Animal
## That Can't Fall Down

**Mackenzie and I couldn't get to the museum** until nearly three-thirty in the afternoon. We went straight up to the fifth floor, and I knocked on Gardner's open office door. He looked up, surprised, from behind his chrome-and-glass desk.

"Oh, Peter . . . and Mackenzie," he said. "Come in. What can I do for you?"

"We need to talk to you," I said.

"I'm a little busy. . . ." Gardner started.

I cut him off. "This is important."

"Oh," Dr. Gardner said, curiously. "In that case, do sit down." He was dressed informal-preppie today, in a dark-blue sports jacket and red-and-blue-striped tie. Mackenzie and I sat on the black leather sofa. I watched her eyes sweep over the shelves of art and history books like radar and come to rest on the bull's head and rabbit's foot paperweight. I looked at the frames with Gardner's family photos with everyone in cowpoke gear with new interest.

"We want to talk to you about this," I said, pushing the newspaper article across to him.

Gardner sat motionless for a long while. He didn't pick up the article, simply looked down at it, knowing very well what it was. Finally, he swiveled in his chair and stared out the window to the park.

"Dr. Farr was blackmailing you for years, wasn't she?" I said.

"I would have lost my job," Gardner said, barely audible. "She and I knew the Board of Trustees would have gotten rid of me the moment they found out about anything like this. There would be no way they would have let me continue as the museum director." He cleared his throat. "I have a family. I would have lost so many things. My pension. I would have no health plan. No other museum would take me with a mistake like that. That's what it was. The mistake of a very young man. Three of the children in the crash were permanently crippled. There isn't a day when I don't think about them. About the young lives I've ruined. I've tried to give back, to make amends by my work here—by programs for young people. By special projects . . ."

I glanced at Mackenzie. I knew what she was dying to ask. But she didn't.

To tell the truth, the two of us sat dumbfounded along with Gardner. Finally, I forced the words out. "Did you kill Dr. Farr?" I asked.

"No," he said.

"We found the article in her copy machine," Mackenzie said. "Why would she have been copying it again now?"

"She always sent me a fresh copy from time to time to remind me," Dr. Gardner said. "Usually, it'd be when she was going to ask me to do something else for her. You don't know how many times I had wished she would quit and leave, and when I heard she'd been strangled—when Max came here to my office and told me—my first feeling was of relief."

I decided to get straight to the meat and potatoes. "Where were you when Conchetta was murdered?" I asked.

Gardner looked surprised at my question, like he hadn't expected it at all. "I was having a late working-lunch in my office—actually, with Dr. Mirsky. We were going over details of the gala. The speeches . . ."

"You and Dr. Mirsky were together in this office the whole time?" Mackenzie asked.

"Let me see," Dr. Gardner said. "Well, no. At one point Dr. Mirsky said he had to get a folder from his office—that he'd be right back. He was gone maybe ten minutes—when Max came in to tell me that Dr. Farr had been murdered. I guess I don't have a very good alibi, but I assure you I didn't murder Dr. Farr, and I think you have a nerve to even suggest that. What are you going to do now?" Gardner asked us. "You'll be telling the police about my past?"

Mackenzie kept her eyes on me waiting for me to call the next shot. "I don't know what we're going to do, but I know something I want you to do," I said. "For us."

"What?" Gardner asked.

"We want to see the Ganesh necklace," I said.

"Oh, that's out of the question," Gardner said. "The necklace can't be seen by anyone until the night of the gala, and that's that."

"You've seen it, right?" I said. "And Spiegelman must have seen it, too."

"Of course," Gardner said.

"Can you tell us anything about it?" Mackenzie asked. "Could you at least describe it for us?"

"I suppose that would be all right," he said. "It's a rather colossal piece—nearly two feet of jewels and gold mesh. And let's see," he went on, remembering it, "it has a series of seven three-inch-long crescents each topped by a massive blazing white diamond. Each diamond is exactly thirty-six carats. Each is priceless."

"Why is it called the Ganesh necklace?" Mackenzie asked.

"Actually, the literal translation of the Indian name of the necklace is 'Ganesh Travels Around the World,'" Gardner said. "There are rectangles of solid gold which hang from each of the crescents. The rectangles are a series of intricately carved scenes, such as Ganesh walking through a town of bamboo huts. In another, Ganesh is riding a tiger through a swamp. In yet another he is swimming across a sea. It's exactly what you'd expect. Scenes of Ganesh traveling around the world."

"And no one besides you and Spiegelman has seen the necklace?" I asked.

Gardner thought a moment longer. "Let's see," he said, "Dr. Farr asked to see it. Maybe that's why she had dug the article on me out of the files, thinking I might refuse her. She's been to India a great deal. Spiegelman and I didn't want anyone to see the necklace. It is the most amazing piece of jewelry I've ever seen."

"Is it true that the necklace has never before been photographed?" I asked.

"That is the coup for the museum. It will be displayed tomorrow night at our gala for the first time in a thousand years. All the press and TV networks will be here. It is the consummate honor of my entire career that Dr. Spiegelman was able to get the Maharajah and his royal family to release the necklace and allow us to show it."

"The museum in Vancouver must be eating its heart out to have lost Dr. Spiegelman," Mackenzie said.

"I'm certain they are," Gardner said.

I noticed his hands were shaking.

"The responsibility of having to protect the gold and diamonds in a necklace like that must be nerve-racking," I said, watching for his reaction.

"It is," Gardner said. "Well, Peter and Mackenzie, what are you going to do? Are you going to report my past to the police?" Gardner pressed us. "I was hoping you would extend me the courtesy of talking it over with your father before you do."

I'll bet you were hoping that, I thought. By the time I got my dad on the phone in the jungles of Sumatra, Gardner would have a whole mess of time in which to knock me and Mackenzie off, too.

"We have to think a few things over, Dr. Gardner," I said.

"For sure," Mackenzie said. She clutched her fake-leopard shoulder bag like it was a security blanket.

"I understand," Gardner said.

We stared at each other for a moment. Mackenzie turned and started off, with me right after her. As we left the museum by way of the 79th Street exit, I heard Mackenzie half-wheeze, half-whisper through her teeth: "Did he kill her or not?"

"Let's just say that he and Mirsky don't exactly have airtight alibis," I said.

"Right. Each is like a witness that the other had the window on time to have murdered Farr. And, of course, it could still be Spiegelman, you know—and we need to check if Congers has an alibi."

The mimosa trees surrounding the museum were filled with chattering swallows preparing to migrate. I started counting the cracks between the slabs of the sidewalk, which drives me nuts because sometimes I have trouble turning it off.

"I can't imagine Mirsky wrinkling his clothes choking

anyone," I said, finally. "And Congers, I think her talent for evil leaves off at planting centipedes. She probably drops balloons filled with maple syrup on people, too. I just think there's so much more here than meets the eye." I lifted my gaze to the gargoyles perched high on the San Remo apartment house. "And, only Gardner and Spiegelman know the combination to the gem vault. They're the only two who could get at the necklace!"

"It does sound like the most beautiful necklace in the world," Mackenzie said. "Did you see the awe in Garnder's eyes as he described it—like he was talking about something made by a wizard or a god."

"What a shame it's a fake," I said.

Mackenzie stopped instantly and put her hands on her hips. "What do you mean it's a fake?" she practically shouted at me. "How could you possibly know that?"

"Look, in India Ganesh is a god," I told her. "He's their most important god. Everyone there knows the legend of Ganesh traveling around the world—it's Ganesh walking around his parents. There's no way anyone's going to make a necklace and completely change the Ganesh legend—certainly not in India. It'd be sacrilegious. That necklace has got to be a fake. Don't you see? That's why Farr was murdered! It's got something to do with the necklace being a fake!"

I took Mackenzie by the arm and marched her on down the street with me. The rush-hour crowd began to wash over us: women in overalls and halters; the delivery boys on bikes; men carrying pet cages and Rollerblading. Burglar alarms on two cars were triggered, and buses with huge underwear ads flew by.

"There's several places that specialize in creating great-looking imitations," I said. "Fabulous Fakes, they call them. The Ganesh shown in that necklace isn't sharp and cool, he's a drudge. Whoever had that necklace made didn't know beans about Indian religion or folklore."

"You're right," Mackenzie said. "The Ganesh Gardner described isn't doing anything clever at all. If Dr. Farr knew it, that'd be a good reason for someone to knock her off. Someone who was afraid of her turning him or her in."

"Or someone who couldn't stand her blackmailing anymore," I said. "The article on Gardner would be small pickings, because Farr had seen the necklace. With her knowledge of India she would have known the necklace is a fake."

"But why wouldn't Spiegelman realize it was a fake, too, if he's this big Indian antiquities honcho?" Mackenzie said.

I thought that over a minute. "Because he might be a fake, too," I said.

"A fake making a fake?"

"Could be. What we've got to figure out is why would anyone go to the trouble of creating a replica to replace the real valuable necklace and not even do it right?"

"What we've got to do is find out more about Spiegelman," Mackenzie said.

"Bingo, again!"

My cell phone rang. It was Jesus.

"What's happening," I said. Jesus started talking but his voice on the phone had an echo because of the tall buildings around me. I ran a ways to the open courtyard of the Fourth Universal Society Church. There the expanse of Central Park cleared up the signal.

"I finished checking who at the museum was in India during the last few years. You know who traveled there the most?"

"Who?"

"Farr," Jesus said.

"Oh, yes—Gardner told us she's been there a lot."

"Right. She was in Rajasthan dozens of times, usually collecting insects. Spiders. She's been to Bombay and the American Embassy School in Delhi. Bangladesh. The swamps in the south . . ."

Mackenzie had her ear glued to the phone with me. "Of course," she said. "Farr's wolf spiders, the ones we saw in her lab, are from India. I've seen a special on those on the Discovery Channel."

"And we know Farr wasn't shy," I said. "I'm sure she weaseled invitations into every palace in every province. She must have pulled strings and managed to get herself invited to the one in Rajasthan."

"She *did* see the real necklace," Mackenzie said.

Jesus's voice crackled and echoed again. "What are you talking about?"

"Fakes!" I said. "We're talking about fakes!"

## Evil Eye

**"Hey, how's it going?"** Santo, one of the Dominican doormen asked as I came through the lobby's revolving door at 30 Lincoln Plaza. It was eight o'clock and the whole place had a buzz more like a luxury hotel than a residential apartment building.

"I'm always the last to know," I said.

Santo winked. "I don't think so."

I waved to Louie, the concierge, and headed for the bank of express elevators. Up in my apartment I left the lights off for a few minutes and drank in the night view of the Chagall murals at the opera house across the street. A lot of the singers and orchestra members lived in our building, as well as half of the on-camera news team from CBS.

At nine-thirty that night Mackenzie called. "I talked things over with my mom," she said. "She thinks we should just tell the police everything we know about the case. All that grisly past about Gardner and why we think he knocked off Farr. Just tell them everything and let them run with it from here. Well, at least *stroll* with it."

"She's probably right," I said numbly.

"Mom knows the cops may be slow, but they'll find out soon enough that Tom is really innocent and let him go. It just takes a while for all the paperwork and memos to filter down. She says we should let Lieutenant Krakowski finish the case, and that we shouldn't go up to the museum anymore until your father gets back and this whole thing is over. She thinks it's gotten too dangerous."

"Okay."

"It's best."

"Yes."

"We did all that we could. . . ."

Mackenzie had that *I'm going to hang up soon* tone in her voice. She usually got that when we'd be up too late talking on our cell phones and watching Jay Leno or a nature special on meerkats or hyenas. "But you know," she piped up, "the thing that puzzles me is why the real murdering crook hasn't left town. It makes you really wonder, if the priceless Ganesh necklace has already been replaced, why isn't the killer on a plane to Buenos Aires or Rio?"

"Greed—as usual," I finally said. "Two good reasons would be that he's a little crazy, and also that he hasn't finished replacing everything he's had his heart set on yet."

"Like the Star of India sapphire!" Mackenzie said. "Or the South African diamond collection. Or the

Sloane broach and the British Royal ruby and opal ring. Gardner and Spiegelman know everything worth taking from the entire museum gem displays, and they've got the combination to the vault!"

I thought out loud. "The good news is that the killer has got to think we're dummies—that we wouldn't know the Ganesh necklace was a phony. He thinks I'll be worried about my dad's job and we'll actually just shut up about everything until he gets back. I guess Gardner must really be certifiable."

"Could be," Mackenzie said. "I mean, for years he's been taking orders from the Board of Trustees, right? Years of buying and trading and displaying some of the most famous jewels of all history. A guy like that has got to fill up with envy. Gardner's the one, right?"

"I think so. I read about types like him," I said.

"Me, too," Mackenzie said. "Fine art thieves who will stop at nothing to surround themselves with paintings and jewels that are so famous and priceless they could never sell them."

"Yes," I agreed. "They steal them or bid for them on the black market and then buy a hacienda on a pampa somewhere in South America and live with the treasures. They sit alone with them in a room and light candles—and tremble at touching them. It takes a real maniac, someone more twisted than Silas Marner to want to live like that. To give up his country and family and friends, and finish out the rest of a lifetime in some kind of sick, secret solitude."

"Do you want Kim to call the lieutenant and fill her in?" Mackenzie asked. "I'll get on the extension to make sure she gets it right."

"You might as well," I said. "Krakowski would shriek at me like a banshee if I tried to tell her anything."

I hung up and went to bed early hoping I could just put everything out of my mind. Sometimes going to bed is the best thing I can do because my brain works out a lot of problems while I lie there and stare at the ceiling. My mind just sort of spins like an out-of-control movie until it synthesizes all the weird stuff I see every day.

I finally got to sleep, but then the dreams started. First there were a lot of rude sentries, all of whom looked like Lieutenant Krakowski, leaping out at me from behind trees and yelling at me. At first I thought they were all irate exotic dancers. Then for a while I dreamed I was walking through a whole landscape of Chinese box puzzles. You know, where you open one box and all you find in it is another box, and another, and another and so on until you lose your sanity. Usually I have that dream when my nose is stuffed up.

In the morning, just before I woke up, I had another dream where Krakowski was running after me with a chain saw. It was really weird because she cut off my arms and legs and then she tried to glue them back on me again. I knew where that dream came from, because I'd been reading one of my father's books about medicine men. "The sign that you might be a shaman," the book said, "was if you dream of being dismembered by heavenly spirits and then put back together again." The thought of Lieutenant Krakowski being a heavenly spirit made me laugh out loud.

I got up, dressed, wolfed down a bowl of Cap'n Crunch topped with almonds and M&Ms, and went to school. When I caught up with Mackenzie during fourth-period lunch, she told me Kim had spoken to the police and that they were going to pass the information along to Krakowski. If you ask me, Mackenzie and I walked through the rest of the day like somnambulists on Robitussin. I just couldn't feel very much about anything, even Spalding Kazinski nagging and complaining about how little we'd done on our folklore project.

After school Mackenzie walked me home. On the way, we put in a call to Jesus and asked him to run a check on Spiegelman. There was hardly anything on him in the museum database, but I knew Jesus would be able to dig up stuff on him from Vancouver. Mac and I didn't even stop for burgers at the Cosmic Café. We just went home and decided to wait to hear from him.

"I guess once the press photographs the necklace tonight, it'll go out on all the news wires. Somebody will spot it as a fake and really blow the whistle. Gardner's got to know that."

"I suppose so," I said. "We ought to check all the

airlines and see who's taking off for where. It wouldn't hurt to see if anyone's leaving town."

"They won't give you that information over the phone."

"I know."

"I hope Krakowski figures everything out," Mackenzie said. "She's probably already totally involved in some other crime like setting up stakeouts to break a diaper ring or something."

"Probably," I said.

I went up to my apartment. Aunt Doris stopped by with half a sausage white-cheese pizza and a box of Entenmann's cupcakes with little sugar jack-o'-lanterns on them. I wasn't halfway through a slice before she asked me if I knew that a study had been done and it discovered that "ninety-three percent of people are surprised by their own death." After that news, I told her I wasn't hungry.

When she finally left, I started to walk around the apartment for a while, then I put on the television and watched a rerun of *How to Survive a Bear Attack* and channel-surfed between the second half of *Gumby: The Movie* and an infomercial on how to have abs like Jean-Claude Van Damme used to have if I bought a skateboard contraption for four payments of $37.99.

It was after eight o'clock when I strolled out to the kitchen and made myself a glass of chocolate milk with a cocoa mix that had awful little fake dried marshmallows in it. As I sipped the cocoa, I drifted back down the hall like a disembodied spirit. The door to my dad's bedroom was open. The light spill from the hallway lamp cut across the room and fell on a picture of my mother in a silver frame on a bed table.

"It takes ten years to get over the death of a mother," Aunt Doris had told me at my mom's funeral. "I don't really mean 'get over,'" she had added, "but you know what I'm saying." I wonder where a lot of aunts get that talent for saying things that haunt you and bug you and drive you out of your gourd.

For a while I lay across my father's bed wondering why I couldn't stop thinking about the murder and the Ganesh necklace. Why couldn't I just let it go like anyone else in their right mind would? Kim was right. Things had gotten too perilous. It was a matter for the police, not me and Mackenzie.

Then I figured out why I *couldn't* let it go. My mom was looking at me from her photograph. There were so many things I had remembered her telling me, but one of them was churning over and over in my mind: "It's never the easy way," my mom had once told me. "It's never that way. It just isn't . . ."

Whatever, I felt restless. I began to get it through my thick skull that once the photos of the fake necklace hit the news and wire services, someone is going to notice it. Whoever the killer is will have to escape right after the unveiling. I got up off the bed. I knew what I'd have to do. I went to the phone in the living room and dialed Mackenzie's number. After three rings, she answered.

"What?

"Remember the dress you wore to Jennifer Leibowitz's bat mitzvah?" I said.

"Of course I remember it. It was last weekend."

"Well, put it on."

"Now?"

"Yes."

"Why?"

"Because we're going to the gala."

"Are you nuts?"

"Yes," I said. "And I'm picking you up in ten minutes."

Mackenzie was waiting out in front of the Riggses' brownstone when I pulled up in the cab. She looked cool in her red cocktail dress that didn't have much material on the top or very much material on the bottom, either. As usual, she was clutching tightly to her fake-leopard-skin shoulder bag as she slid into the backseat next to me.

"I hope you know what you're getting us into," she said.

"Not quite."

"I figured."

The moment the taxi turned up Broadway we could see the lights of the benefit. There were four of the Laser Sky-beam rental trucks parked in front of the

JAMES BUCHANAN HIGH SCHOOL
ILL — IDS# 286-A13
6773 Ft. Loudon Road
Mercersburg, PA 17236

museum and flashing their rays high into the sky like the gala was some sort of a big Hollywood opening.

"We're late, you know," Mackenzie said, as she adjusted the rhinestone straps on the pair of her mother's shoes she'd borrowed for the night. "All the best hors d'oeuvres will have been gobbled up."

"We're not going for the food," I reminded her. "We're not even invited." I dialed Jesus on my cell phone. I had already had one catch-up call with him that night.

Jesus answered on the first ring. "What, P.C.?"

"We're in the cab now heading for the gala," I said. The taxi driver was a little man with glasses like petri dishes and wearing an enormous white turban. He was watching us in the rearview mirror when Mackenzie shoved her head next to mine so she could hear Jesus.

"Jesus, I need you to check out a few other things that have to do with Mirsky, Congers, and Spiegelman," I said. "Check for any Caucasians that might have been found dead in Rajasthan around September fifth. I figure that's about when Spiegelman had picked up the Ganesh necklace. Also, call the Bombay police about any murders or accidents, too, because the Bombay airport was Spiegelman's port of entry and exit."

"But I was thinking about it—it couldn't be Spiegelman," Mackenzie said. "It wouldn't make any sense for an expert in Indian antiquities to commission anyone to make an incorrect replica of the Ganesh necklace."

"Unless our Dr. Spiegelman really *isn't* Dr. Spiegelman," Jesus said, already with the program.

Mackenzie cried out. "You mean it's possible Conchetta saw that the necklace was fake, so therefore she had to be killed?"

"Look," I said, "it can't hurt to check out every angle. Make sure we haven't missed anything, Jesus."

"Gotcha," Jesus said.

"Hold it, Jesus," I said, grabbed by an afterthought.

"What?"

"Call the museum in Vancouver. Find out if there have been any irregularities on the staff other than Spiegelman leaving for a new job. Sniff out anything you can. We need this stuff *yesterday*."

"You got it," Jesus said.

"And ask them to fax one of their file pictures of Dr. Spiegelman to my dad's office."

I flipped my phone closed as the cab stopped in front of the museum. A red carpet stretched from the curb up the expanse of cement steps to the entrance. Several photographers came running to see if any more society celebs were arriving. They held their cameras with flashes high in the air and ready as Mackenzie and I stepped out of the Yellow Cab. It took the guys a moment before they groaned and let their cameras fall limp from their shoulder straps.

"It's *nobody*," one of them said, right in our faces.

"We're somebody! You're the nobodies! Get a life!" Mackenzie shot back at them as we pushed past and started running up the steps. "I mean, what if we were sensitive?" she whispered in my ear.

Max and Patience were posted at the door to make certain nobody got in without an invitation. Except us, of course.

"Hey," Max said. "Where are you two going?"

"Dr. Gardner's expecting us," I said.

"Hi, Patience," Mackenzie said as we sailed by and then cut across the floor of the rotunda. I really hadn't lied very much about Gardner expecting us. Somewhere in the back of his mind he must have known he hadn't seen the last of us by a long shot.

We cut past the sixty-three-foot-long canoe in the center of the Northwest Coast Indian exhibit, past the Mollusks of Our World, and through the Hall of Human Biology and Evolution.

"It's got to be Spiegelman or Gardner," I said. "I'm going to start with Gardner."

"What are you going to say to him?" Mackenzie wanted to know.

"You'll see."

"It's going to cause trouble, isn't it?"

"That's a positive."

As we turned the corner of the meteorite exhibits we could see the gala dinner was already underway. Each of the dining tables was lit by candlelight, and brilliant-color lasers bounced off several of the featured display cases. The Ganesh necklace and several of the other important gems in the museum collection were in special high-tech displays. *It's too late for that*, I felt like telling someone.

A string orchestra was playing "They Call it That Jersey Bounce," and then switched to the waltz from *The Merry Widow* as Mackenzie and I entered the Hall of Minerals and Gems. Several couples were dancing on a small rectangle in front of the orchestra. Mirsky was animatedly performing for his entire ringside table. Congers was dressed in what looked like woven aluminum, and giggling like she had too much special sauce. In fact, her whole table of café society were laughing their heads off about something. She was probably privately celebrating something like, "Oh, great, they couldn't pin that centipede rap on me."

"Where's Spiegelman?" Mackenzie wondered.

A few moments later, we heard a whirring sound cut through the din of the conversations. I caught a glimpse of Spiegelman holding court in front of the display that featured the Patricia Emerald. He had that massive smile slicing his face in half, and was saying, "This emerald was found in the Colombian Andes mountains in 1920. It weighs six hundred and thirty-two carats, making it one of the largest emeralds in the world. . . ."

Spiegelman's cheeks looked extra puffy and smooth

tonight, and he zipped his motorized wheelchair left and right to emphasize his remarks. He still looked much too big for it, like when you see big Americans sit in those tiny bus seats that were all made and manufactured in Japan—or like my aunt Doris in a dodgem car.

We spotted Gardner.

"You wait here," I told Mackenzie. "And, as they say, buckle your safety belt—it's going to be a bumpy ride."

She scrunched up her nose. "Be careful."

I wiggled my way between the crowded tables. Gardner was seated at the head table with all the most important guests, including the Borough President of Manhattan and some woman I'd seen before who owns U.S. Steel. Their table was right between the case with the Ganesh necklace and another that held the Star of India sapphire. I had read all about it years ago, how it was discovered three hundred years ago in Sri Lanka and was even once stolen from the museum. Some guy by the name of "Murph the Surf" had masterminded the burglary, but the crooks got caught and the gem was returned to the museum eight weeks later.

Gardner stopped midsentence when he saw me weaving through the mob toward him. Everyone at his table turned to follow his gaze as he excused himself and got up to head me off.

"What is it, Peter?" Gardner said. He kept a smile on his face so no one would know he was worried about anything, but I saw otherwise. "I didn't know you were coming tonight."

"Mackenzie and I needed to tell you something," I whispered. "Something really important about the Ganesh necklace."

"What is it, Peter?"

"It's a fake," I said. "I really think the Ganesh necklace is a fake."

Gardner stared at me a moment looking really puzzled, but, I thought, not particularly shocked. "What a strange thing to say," he said, finally.

"Chances are that it's not real," I said. "Someone who didn't know anything about Indian antiquities had it duplicated. You know, did a switcheroo." I waited for his reaction. After a moment he started laughing. He was still amused when I heard a familiar sound.

*Whirrrrrrrr.*

Spiegelman rolled by us in his chair. Gardner waved him to brake. "Dr. Spiegelman, were you able to pick up your airline tickets okay this afternoon?"

"Just fine," Spiegelman said. "Thanks for letting me duck out to get them."

"Where are you going?" I asked.

"I have a sister and nephew in Florida . . ."

"Weekeewatchie, or whatever that is, right, Dr. Spiegelman?"

"Yes," Spiegelman said. "I'm taking them fishing and parasailing. I can use a little vacation—what, with the gala, I've been going 'round the clock for the museum."

"Well," Gardner said, gathering us like players in a football huddle, "let's send you off with a laugh. It appears Hawke's boy here has become an expert in Indian culture as well as being a detective. Peter says the Ganesh necklace is a fake."

Gardner laughed louder than I've ever heard him. I didn't even want to look at Spiegelman, but I think it was because I didn't hear him joining in the laughter that I glanced up into his weird cookie-dough countenance. What I saw was Spiegelman's face stiffened and enraged into a hate mask. His eyes looked like those of a maniac and were locked on me. I realized that I had made a mistake.

"Well," I said, forcing a little smile. "I guess I have to be going now."

I turned and squeezed my way back through the swarm of seated guests. One table had just gotten its entree and were munching on what looked like dried-out chicken breasts on a plate with radishes sculptured to look like roses. I knew Gardner wouldn't follow me to draw me out on anything, and I knew for sure Spiegelman wouldn't be able to drive his wheelchair through the mob.

"What's the matter?" Mackenzie asked as I raced back to her.

"The killer isn't Gardner," I said. "It's Dr. S."

"How do you know?"

"I know," I said. "And then some." I flipped open my

cell phone but couldn't get a dial tone this deep inside the steel and cement walls of the museum. Mackenzie's phone wouldn't be any better. "Go to Max's office," I said. "Tell him what's going on."

"Max may have a gun."

"Not a chance," I said. "It's against Museum rules. Call Krakowski. The police. And if they don't answer call the fire department. Anybody!" I realized my nerves were getting the best of me. "Tell Krakowski that Spiegelman's our murderer and is going to clear out of here tonight. It's not going to be Disney World. It's going to be Brazil, where all those crooked accountants go. I know it!"

"I don't want to call her," Mackenzie said. "You know she'll just start yelling and say we're nuts."

"*Do* it!" I said, spinning and heading for the elevators.

Mackenzie looked freaked. She put her hands on her hips. "And where do you think you're going?"

"My dad's office!"

"Are you demented? We should both just get out of here."

The elevator doors opened. I got in and pointed Mackenzie toward Max's office. "Chop chop."

The doors started to close as Mackenzie looked ready to shove her foot between them. "That lunatic will come after you," she practically spit at me and punched the door. "He will!"

A moment later the elevator was traveling down.

## Making a Killing

**With the museum closed for the gala,** only a few naked lightbulbs lit the expanse of the planetarium lobby when I reached the lower level. In Hallway C the night-lights were recessed, casting a crisscross of shadows on the walls. A number of manikins and artifacts for changes in the medieval exhibit had been hauled out to be cleaned and readied by the custodian and installation staffs. The armored knights, the swords and maces, and "galloping" steeds would be moved into place in the morning. Once I had watched a team of the museum's taxidermists and sculptors transform the dead body of a Belmont Racetrack stallion into a furious equine mummy.

I thought of Tom as I passed the barricaded door of Conchetta's lab. Beyond, passing the closed door of her office, I could only remember Tom's face. His trembling and crying out. I didn't want to fail him. I just didn't. *It won't be long now and you'll be out.* I wished I could send my thoughts to him. *We know who the killer is. You'll be okay. Your mind will be fine again.*

I reached my dad's office, unlocked the door, and went in. I flicked the light switch but only one of the fluorescent tubes in the ceiling light sputtered on. I jumped up and slapped the plastic underbelly of the fixture a few times. That was usually good enough to get them all aglow.

But not tonight.

My mother's curtain of sea horses and jellyfish hung limp on the far wall. Mackenzie had been right, of course. The killer could follow me down, but there was too much to do. I tried my dad's phone but the service was suspended as it always was between nine at night and six in the morning. The company gave the museum a cheaper corporate rate for that. There were the fumes from a pine cleaner left from a recent floor-washing. They burned in my nostrils as I tried my cell phone. Its NO SERVICE sign flashed for a long while before a line opened up.

I pressed the automatic dial button for Jesus. While the signal connected and rang, I checked my dad's fat, gray fax machine that stood to one side near the cluttered desk in the corner. The fax-receiving bin was empty.

Jesus answered. "Did you get my messages?"

"No."

"I couldn't get through to the police in Rajasthan, but I found what you wanted from the cops in Bombay. The police there said an adult Caucasian male 'floater' was found in the Ganges on September twelfth. I checked the dates. Gardner and Spiegelman were in that city. Gardner had finished making the arrangements on several other objects in the museum there, and met up with Spiegelman after he'd picked up the necklace in Rajasthan."

"What else did the Bombay cops say?"

"The 'floater' had atrophied legs."

"The dead man was a cripple?"

"Right. And he'd been *strangled*, not drowned."

The phone signal faded quickly and then cut out like it often did. I tried the redial button, but couldn't get a tone.

I was alone and in silence, and could feel my own heartbeat. My nose had grown numb from the smell of disinfectant, and I stared at the fax machine wondering if Jesus had spoken to anyone in Vancouver.

There came sounds.

I recognized the noisy arrival of the freight elevator at the end of the hall. It was followed by a clanging as the elevator gate was manually opened. My belly drew into a chill, hard knot as another moment of silence followed.

Then a *whirring*.

I strained to hear what I knew was coming. The noise of the motor was fitful at first, and I realized the wheelchair was being maneuvered past the ghastly silhouettes of knights and swords. I had spotted an iron maiden and torture boots and a device called the "Scavenger's Daughter." It was an English inquisition device that could compress the human body, causing ruptures, hemorrhages, and broken bones.

In a moment, the large man in the wheelchair was in the office doorway, a small blanket tossed across his lap as though he had a chill.

"Hello, Dr. Spiegelman," I said, my tongue growing thick and numb.

"Yes," Spiegelman said. He shifted and drove his chair over the slightly raised aluminum threshold, then stopped where he still blocked the sole exit.

"I'm glad you came down," I said.

"May I ask why?"

My eyes were burning now, and I squirmed in my clothes. The tuxedo felt wet and rumpled and its bow tie was too tight around my throat. "I think we should talk about you giving yourself up to the police. You need to talk to them. You really need to do that, Dr. Spiegelman."

Spiegelman peered at me kindly. He looked pleasant, like we'd just run into each other at a Shop Rite and were talking about what kind of frozen pizzas or chicken pot pies we were buying. Pepperoni or sausage. Full piecrust or half. "What a bizarre thought," he said. "Why would you want me to do a thing like that?"

"Because you killed Dr. Farr, sir," I said. I didn't know why I called him sir. It was like I wanted to speak more words. To draw my sentences out and soften everything I would have to say. I think I wanted time to stand still.

Dr. Spiegelman didn't look quite as amused now. "You're confused," he said. "I believe it was your friend who was seen choking poor Conchetta to death, not me. You did say Tom was your friend, didn't you? I realize how it must affect your judgment. By the way, where is your hyper girlfriend?"

I watched the avuncular mask melting away from his face. A sternness had replaced his saccharineness, like he was a geometry teacher displeased at having to repeat a corollary.

"Oh, yes," I said. My hands began to shake, and Spiegelman's eyes locked on the weakness like a hawk. "Tom was seen with his hands around Conchetta's throat," I went on, "but you had already killed her. We've known for quite a while about the drug you gave Tom. We know you programmed him and we know the triggers. So do the police. Mackenzie's gone to get the cops. They'll be here any moment."

He knew I wasn't too sure about that.

Spiegelman dropped his hands down to his lap.

"We don't know about your extensive training in hocus-pocus or brainwashing or whatever your background is," I said. "There was no record of it because we were checking under Spiegelman's name. Whoever you are, you probably did a stint in some special unit of the Canadian Army. Maybe you trained dogs. The techniques are the same, sort of, aren't they?"

"What an amusing theory that is, P.C. I hope you

don't mind, but I must say if you're going to be a detective like you seem to be telling everyone, you're not going to be a very good one. You'll find out that courts and the police don't act on zany theories like yours. They need what is called hard evidence, not some loser of a kid clumsily sending up absurd trial balloons."

The phone rang and he whirred his chair in a half circle. The blanket fell from his lap to reveal the clawed workman's hammer laying there. He looked down on it as though he'd just spotted fallen dandruff or a small gravy stain.

On the second ring, the phone signal automatically switched to the fax. The machine answered, and the beeps sounded as the machines began to talk to each other. A moment later and the printing stylus flew rapidly across and back, back and across, until the image of a man began to rise up into the receiving bin. It was the image of a small, thin handicapped man smiling in front of an Indian statue of a goddess with hundreds of arms. The imposter stared at the picture.

"Is that hard evidence enough, do you think?" I asked. "And if it isn't, the fake Ganesh necklace upstairs that you commissioned certainly will be. It won't be difficult for the police to track down who made it for you."

"Oh, this gets crazier, doesn't it?"

"Not really. There was so much about you that bothered Mackenzie and me from the beginning. You were too big for your wheelchair. Of course you *would* be—it wasn't yours. You lied about having been in Conchetta's office. Probably the truth of it was that you came running whenever she jangled her bell, since she knew from the start that both you and the necklace were fakes."

A veil of hate descended over Spiegelman's eyes. "She was a terrible, greedy person," he said, sounding as if his hands were around her throat and he was choking her again.

"Whoever you are, you knew the real Dr. Spiegelman, that's for sure. You knew a great deal about him and a lot about gemstones, but nothing about Indian antiquities—and you saw a chance to be very, very rich."

Spiegelman's imposter put the wheelchair in gear and began to creep it toward me. His right hand grasped the hammer, but my instincts told me to keep talking. "Of course, the moment you laid your eyes on the real Ganesh necklace, you knew you had a problem following through on the rest of your master plan—to make off with the centerpieces of this museum's entire gem collection? That was it, correct? Tonight's gala was your last shot. With all the press here you knew it would only be a matter of time before someone, somewhere, recognized it was a fake."

The imposter placed his feet on the floor and began to stand, lifting the hammer high into the air.

My voice was breaking now. "We know you killed the real Dr. Spiegelman in India soon after he accepted the necklace from the royal family. I can imagine how surprised you were when you took the necklace from him and you saw what the real Ganesh necklace looked like—how different it was from the fake you already had made—but it was much too late to change it before meeting up with Gardner."

My hands were behind me now. They felt the curtain on the wall, and then instinct clicked in. I tore at the curtain on the wall, whirling it between me and the killer. It was in the air like a fluttering cape between a bullfighter and a bull. But the curtain fell, and now there was nothing between me and the giant in front of me.

There was a scream from the doorway. "Get away from him!" Mackenzie said.

"It's over," came the strident voice of someone behind her in a colorful sweater.

Mackenzie stepped aside and there was Lieutenant Krakowski with her pistol drawn. "Drop the hammer," she ordered. Two other policemen rushed into the room. The imposter dropped the hammer as the cops grabbed him, handcuffed him, and marched him out. He was screaming at us. Screaming.

Mackenzie ran to my side and hugged me. Krakowski stared at us like a prison warden. "You kids are going to be a lot of trouble, aren't you?" she said almost viciously. "A lot of trouble."

"Yes, Lieutenant Krakowski," I said. "We are."

## Death Is Nature's Way of Saying "Howdy"

**It was almost two weeks later** before things got sort of back to normal for Mackenzie and me. My dad came back from Sumatra. Mac and I had gone out to Kennedy Airport to meet him at the International terminal. He's easy to spot in the distance because he looks like Harrison Ford with a short beard, that is if Harrison Ford spent a little too much time at Burger King or White Castle.

Dad gave us a big wave as he came through Customs. He was waving a copy of the *International Herald Tribune*, which had an article about Spiegelman and the Ganesh necklace.

"Gardner called and told me all about it," he said giving us a big hug. "I'm so proud of you both believing in Tom—trusting in your instincts about a friend. Gardner said if you hadn't uncovered the whole hypnosis scam, Tom would have been convicted of murder and sent to prison. Possibly executed."

"Probably," I said.

"Yes," Mackenzie agreed.

To be truthful, we had hoped Gardner didn't tell Dad too much so that he'd be worried about us and our dawning detective careers. We had told Gardner if he didn't tell Dad about all the chances we took, that we wouldn't tell him or anyone about the school accident from his past. Mackenzie and I had thought it over very carefully and we decided Gardner had suffered enough and was doing some really good works for kids now.

Mackenzie and I continued to play catch-up with Dad on the cab ride back from Kennedy. "The cops finally ran a check on the marks around Conchetta's neck and found out they matched the real killer's hands," I said. "There were marks from a school ring, a lot of specifics they would never have checked closely if it was left up to them. It's really scary how the police never look for anything beyond the obvious. All they seem to salivate over is dreaming about their next pay hike or safe cooping nest."

"Right," Mackenzie agreed.

"Hey, you two, don't be so cynical," my dad said. "There are some detectives out there who are just like you. They have dedication and talent, too. A voice inside of themselves that tells them when something is wrong about a case—that someone isn't being truthful, or that a piece of hard evidence isn't what it seems to be. But what a great job you did."

"The imposter's name turned out to be Louis Bossier," Mackenzie said. "He used to work with

Spiegelman. Bossier finally confessed when the body found in Bombay was positively identified as Spiegelman. Bossier also fingered the black market dealer. . . ."

"His 'fence' . . ."

"Right, his fence," Mackenzie said, rolling her eyes. "If Bossier had done a little more homework on Ganesh he wouldn't have ordered such a dull phony necklace made up. He had put out feelers and found a little old couple in Seattle who create really nice terrific fakes for a lot of crooks."

"Speaking of homework," my dad said, "what's happened to your schoolwork through all of this?"

"Hey," I said. "We got the top marks in our English class."

"Right," Mackenzie chimed in. "We've got this new best friend Spalding—he runs around with T-shirts that say things like 'Stamp Out Philately'—anyway, we did this project with him and we all got an A+."

Spalding had turned in an eight-by-ten of me, Mackenzie, and the Ganesh necklace that had been in the newspapers and on TV. There was a photo, too, of the murderer with his weird cookie-dough face—and if you think Wendy Fillerman didn't have another nasty crack or two to make about us and cadavers, you're mistaken.

We had brought Dad a box of Godiva chocolates out to greet him when he got off the plane and finished with

Customs. He had brought us each an Indonesian ape mask. Naturally, Mackenzie and I put them on and started yelling out of the window of the cab. The driver thought we were really nuts, but my dad's used to us. He had helped save more than fifty-three orangutans by relocating them to preserves in the Barisan mountains. He said he might have to make a return trip soon because some fossilized human bones were found somewhere between the port of Djambi and Mt. Kerintji.

"Can we go with you?" I asked. Mackenzie and I hadn't been anywhere with him since Madagascar the last winter.

"That could be a positive," Dad said, winking.

Mackenzie and I had spent most of the time since breaking the murder case striking as low a profile as possible in school and taking walks in the park.

The good news was that Tom was out of jail, deprogrammed, and back at work at the museum. He still had to see a therapist for a while, and he'd tell us all the crazy questions he was being asked, like, "When you're watching a rock video on TV and the audience applauds, do you think the audience is applauding for you?" We did manage to get him out to the park a few times with us. Sure, the hood with the chrysanthemum hair popped up here and there, but it was clear he had only been chatting up Tom to find out the lay of the land at the museum.

"Do you think the Chrysanthemum Kid is the one

who's been stealing the office stuff?" Mackenzie asked.

"Do bears live in the woods?" I said.

"Gotcha."

I think what kept Mackenzie and me sane most was going to our favorite knoll near the boat pond. As usual, we always brought the weirdest questions we could think of. We talked about murder and death a lot. One day we did nothing but sit there and experiment opening and closing our hands as fast as we could for a couple of minutes because I'd read that the feeling you get is the same as rigor mortis because you build up lactic acid. Other topics we talked about were why we itch, why women open their mouths when they apply mascara, and how do the police manage to estimate crowds at soccer riots.

One day we just didn't know what to do at all, so we sat around with Kim on her day off and watched a whole evening of those TV sitcoms that feature a complaining wife, a selfish dumb husband, and loud, nagging parents. I don't think we laughed once.

I guess what we had hoped for most of all from solving the Scream Museum murder case finally happened at our school. Mackenzie and I were in the hallway. Spalding and Wendy and that whole crew of freaky Westside School kids were blabbing during a period change and stumbling around like deranged newborn mice, when there came a familiar sound.

*Whirrrrrrrr.*

The kids all got out of the way as Jesus came rolling down the hall in a state-of-the-art motorized wheelchair that had all the bells and whistles.

"Hey, guys," Jesus called to us. He began to shift and turn the chair in circles, with a big smile plastered across his face. Then he tooted his horn and laughed like I'd never seen him laugh before in his life.

"*See?*" Mackenzie said, putting her hands on her hips and glaring at me.

"I know," I said. "It's a very ill wind that doesn't bring somebody some good."

# CHECK
# OUT
# THE
# NEXT
# P.C. HAWKE
# MYSTERY . . .

# THE SURFING CORPSE • Case #2

## Case #2 began something like this:

Have you ever heard the expression, "There's more to this than meets the eye"? Of course you have. It's an old cliché. But like most clichés, it's got some truth to it.

One time, this Russian guy Potemkin actually built a whole village of fake, prosperous-looking house fronts just to make visitors think things were peachy, when of course they weren't. But don't go thinking Potemkin was the only one. There are all kinds of "Potemkin villages" in life.

For instance, years ago the famous magician David Copperfield made the Statue of Liberty disappear—or did he? It's not too hard to fool the masses.

So what, you ask? Well, when you're a detective—like me, P.C. Hawke, and my friend and colleague, Mackenzie Riggs—separating illusion from reality is your mission. That's why the old cliché "There's more to this than meets the eye" keeps coming back to haunt us.

I mean, you think somebody is dead and buried. You mourn them, maybe you cry, and then you get on with your life.

And then, you see the dead man walking. I don't mean like that movie about death row. I mean *for real*. That's what happened to Mackenzie and me—we actually saw a dead man walking.

Or rather, *surfing*.

As always, recording the truth and nothing but the truth (although sometimes it's difficult to tell what the truth really is)—I am,

*P.C. Hawke*

a.k.a. Peter Christopher Hawke